Local Girls

Local Girls

Alice Hoffman

G. P. Putnam's Sons
New York

This is a work of fiction. The events described are imaginary, and the characters are fictitious and not intended to represent specific living persons.

G. P. PUTNAM'S SONS
Publishers Since 1838
a member of
Penguin Putnam Inc.
375 Hudson Street
New York, NY 10014

Published simultaneously in Canada

These stories first appeared in *Agni Review, Boulevard, Cosmopolitan, Five Points, Glimmer Train, Kenyon Review, Ladies' Home Journal, Redbook, Southwest Review,* and *USA Weekend.*

Library of Congress Cataloging-in-Publication Data

Hoffman, Alice.
Local girls / Alice Hoffman.
p. cm.
ISBN 0-399-14507-9 (acid-free paper)
1. United States—Social life and customs—20th century—Fiction.
I. Title.
PS3558.03447L63 1999 98-50632 CIP
813'.54—dc21

Printed in the United States of America
1 3 5 7 9 10 8 6 4 2

This book is printed on acid-free paper. ♾

BOOK DESIGN BY AMANDA DEWEY

Acknowledgments

The author wishes to thank the editors of the magazines where these stories first appeared. Gratitude always to Elaine Markson, Ron Bernstein, Stacy Creamer, and Phyllis Grann for support and encouragement. Thanks too to Pari Berk and Elizabeth Sheinkman. Thank you to the many health and healing professionals who gave so generously of their time and expertise, especially Dr. Kate Isselbacher, Dr. Susan Pories, Dr. Michael Shortsleeve, Dr. Marjorie Rekant, Dr. Jean Fechheimer, and Dr. Lisa Weissmann. To Mih-Ho Cha, Marilyn Ducksworth, Susan Allison, and Leslie Gelbman, many thanks for many books. For their kindness and good advice, love and appreciation to Suzanne Berger, Sue Standing, Maggie Terris, Pamela Painter, Alexandra Marshall, Donna Conrad, Debi Milligan, Perri Klass, Jill McCorkle, and Mindy Givon. For wise words on a variety of subjects thanks to Dr. Victor Grann, Dr. Michael Seiden, Dr. Andrea Resciniti, Andrew and Lisa Hoffman, Jean Touroff, Ginny Cronin, William Mueller, Bill Callahan, Maryellen Delapine, and Sherry Hoffman. With love to Jake Martin and Wolfe Martin and to Max Hoffman. To Tom Martin, Libby Hodges, and Carol DeKnight, thanks would never be enough, and to the girls I grew up with on Long Island: IOU4ever.

All author profits from this edition
are being donated to breast cancer research
and breast cancer care centers.

To

Jo Ann Hoffman

1950–1996

In Peace

Contents

Dear Diary

One thing I've learned is that strange things do happen. They happen all the time. Today, for instance, my best friend Jill's cat spoke. We were making brownies in the kitchen when we heard it say, *Let me out.* Well, we rushed to the back door and did exactly that. We experienced a miracle and now we're looking for more, although Franconia, the town we live in, is not known for such things. Jill and I have known each other our whole lives. One house separates our houses but we act as if it doesn't exist.

We met before we were born and we'll probably still know each other after we die. At least, that's the way we're planning it.

My mother and I left for Atlantic City so quickly I didn't have time to call Jill. We told people we were on our way to visit an old aunt, but really our departure had something to do with love, or the lack of it, and the aunt doesn't even exist. I know other people whose mothers suddenly pack up when their fathers drink or scream, but for us this is more serious. My mother doesn't do things like go to Atlantic City. She doesn't order room service and cry. She once told me that anyone who gets married had better like herself, because there's nobody else in this world that she'll ever really know, not truly.

We stayed in our room in Atlantic City for three days, and didn't go outside once, thanks to room service. We ate like pigs and didn't even bother to brush our teeth until my mother's cousin Margot, who got a divorce last summer and changed the color of her hair to give herself an emotional lift, came to get us. She drove to New Jersey in the Ford Mustang convertible that she refused to let her ex have, since he'd taken her very soul and raked it over red-hot coals.

"Get dressed right now," she told us.

We were wearing our bathrobes and watching an old cowboy movie, which, for some reason, made my mother cry. Maybe it was all those men on horseback who were so steadfast and loyal. Their own men had disappointed them, but somehow Margot and my mother both had hope for improvement. Frankly, I had more faith in the horses.

"I mean now, Frances," Margot said, and because she meant business, my mother actually dressed and put on some lipstick and we went to a Chinese restaurant where the drinks came with little paper umbrellas, which I kept as a souvenir.

Listen to me, Gretel, Margot told me when we'd gone back to the room to pack and my mother was finally out of earshot. *When a marriage breaks up, it's the children who suffer, so baby, hold on tight.* That's why Margot was relieved that she and Tony had never had children, although she became teary whenever she saw a baby.

"Margot is my best friend, but she's completely full of baloney," my mother whispered as we were throwing our suitcases into the trunk. "Take it all with a grain of salt. Maybe even a whole shaker."

Say what you want about the Mustang, it may be gorgeous, but it has very little trunk space. I had to sit in the back seat with the hair dryer and the makeup case on my lap all the way to Franconia, but that didn't stop me from keeping my fingers crossed and wishing we'd wind up someplace other than home.

We're in Florida for one week, the week when the turtles die on the beach and there are jellyfish in the ocean. As soon as we checked into the hotel, my brother,

Jason, who likes to pretend he's not part of our family, went out to study tide pools and no one has seen him since. My parents are here to try to revitalize their marriage, which seems a pretty impossible feat to all outside observers. *Gretel honey, don't get high hopes,* Margot had already warned me when she took me shopping for a bathing suit, a mission which can give anyone with a less than perfect body a complete nervous breakdown. *When it's over, it's over,* Margot told me, and I had the distinct feeling that she was right.

Long before the plane touched down in Miami we could hear our parents arguing, and at the hotel they locked themselves in their room. If you ask me, working so hard at being married can backfire. It certainly is making my father nastier than usual. Not that his bad temper affects me. I keep my own counsel. I go my own way. I order room service and eat Linzer tortes and shrimp scampi alone in the room I was supposed to be sharing with Jason, not that he was ever planning to show up. Even though I was across the hall from my parents, I could still hear them fighting.

I went out to the beach late, later than I'd be allowed to if anyone knew I was alive. That's where I met Jonathan Rabbit, who is now in love with me. He is known as Jack Rabbit, which makes me laugh out loud. Doesn't it figure that the boy who fell for me would be a rodent? He lives in Atlanta and is in the ninth grade, and frankly he's terribly boring. I let him kiss me once, but believe me, I did not hear bells. I only heard the jellyfish sloshing around in the water and the noisy beat of Jack Rabbit's heart.

Florida didn't do anything for my family, but at least it's starting to be spring. Jill and I are keeping our eyes open for miracles. Jack Rabbit calls me constantly and that is something of a miracle. He writes so often you'd think his fingers would start to cramp up. I bring his letters to school, so everyone is well aware that I have a boyfriend in Atlanta. They'll never meet him. They'll never know it's actually possible for a boy to be so boring you'd agree to kiss him just to get him to shut up. I should get paid to listen to him when he calls on the phone. I should get a dollar fifty an hour. Minimum.

Jill told me that when you're really in love, you know right away. I'm not exactly sure how this happens. Is it like a flash of lightning? Like an angel tapping you on the shoulder? Or is it similar to choosing a puppy? You think you're picking the cutest one, but really you wind up going home with the one who keeps insisting on climbing into your lap. That's how we got our dog, Revolver. We thought he was so crazy about us, but it turned out that Labrador retrievers adore everyone. Well, maybe that's what love is, a state of mind ready to grace anyone willing to accept it. Anyone who cares.

School's out. Hurray. Life, however, is still so boring that I'm writing to Jack Rabbit every day. I go to the pool with Jill and take along my notebook and write until I think I'm going blind, then jump into the deep end. We are not going on vacation because no one in my house is talking to each other, so going anywhere together is definitely out. My brother's on the summer science team at the high school, so he's never home. My father is on an exercise kick and has joined a gym, so he's never around either.

My mother and Margot and I spend a lot of time going to movies. It's dark and it's cool and no one knows if you're crying, except for the person sitting directly beside you. Margot buys me anything I want, even Jordan almonds, which are so terrible for your teeth. She's the kind of person who knows about love. She has men calling her in the middle of the night, but they're all no good, or so she says. Just like Jill, she insists she'll know when she meets the right man. But unlike Jill, she tells me exactly what love's evidence is. *I'll just want to kiss him till I die.* To me, this doesn't sound like something to hope for, but people seem to hope for it all the same.

Jill is camping with her parents, and has sent me a postcard that it has happened. The miracle we've been searching for, the great event, the angel's secret. It's love, it really is. It's the boy in the tent next to hers who she sneaks out to meet after her parents are asleep. I sit on my front stoop while Jill is away and think things over. I've smartened up and am no longer waiting for the mailman. Jack Rabbit isn't writing anymore. He went to camp to be a junior counselor and I guess he broke his arm or fell in love with somebody new. Doesn't it figure that I would miss his letters like crazy? Sometimes I read the old ones late at night, and I wonder what was I thinking when I got them. How could I have thought he was boring? Well, I'm the boring one now. When Jill comes back I may have to lie to her. I may tell her Jack Rabbit died in a canoeing accident. My name was the last word he said, or so they tell me. My name brought him comfort with his last dying breath.

Jill and I are not in the same class at school. We never are. The administration doesn't want people who like each other to be together. They think it builds character when they stick people who hate one another in the same room, day after day, and nobody winds up getting killed or maimed. I'm not supposed to know that Jill's mother is seeing a psychiatrist, just as Jill is not supposed to know my parents are no longer sleeping in the same room. My mother spends her nights on a quilt on my floor, and she doesn't cry until she thinks I'm asleep.

Recently, Margot and I went out for ice cream. We had butterscotch sundaes with vanilla ice cream. Margot asked for my advice. She had spotted my father at an expensive restaurant, the kind he'd never take us to, with some woman she'd never seen before and she didn't know whether or not to tell my mother. I have never been much of a tattletale myself, although I understand that there are times when the truth serves its purpose. This didn't seem to be one of those times. For all we knew, this woman could be some business associate, although Margot and I probably would have both been willing to bet our lives that she wasn't.

Don't tell. That was the advice I came up with. My mother was already crying and sleeping on the floor, what good would the truth do her now? Margot didn't eat any of her sundae, and when she offered it to me I realized I was sick to my stomach. I think I've pretty much figured out that in this world, it's better to stick to hot fudge.

On Halloween Jill wore all black and made ears out of felt which she glued to a plastic headband. She was a black cat. She had a tail that was braided out of three silk scarves. I borrowed thirty silver bangle bracelets from my grandmother. I was a fortune-teller. We should have suspected something when we saw the moon. It was orange and so big we couldn't believe it. It was like we could take one big step, and there we'd be: moon girls who had fallen off the rim of the world. My brother laughed at us. Weren't we a little too old for trick-or-treating? Well of course we were, but we didn't care. We went up and down the block, collecting candy; then we walked beyond the high school through the field so we could smoke cigarettes beside the creek. Jill had stolen the cigarettes from her mother's purse, and I had gotten the matches from my grandmother.

"As long as you're not smoking cigarettes," my grandmother had said to me, which pretty much ruined the whole thing. I couldn't enjoy a single puff. Grandma Frieda was visiting for the weekend and she had the ability to put a hex on any form of high jinks. She was sleeping on my floor too, and it was getting pretty crowded there in my room. I could never find my sneakers. I couldn't find my underwear. Every night, as I fell asleep, I'd hear bits of whispered conversation, and every single one seemed to include the word sorrow.

Jill had been practicing and knew how to blow smoke rings. She was blowing a misty ring when some guys from the high school intent on trouble approached. Jill looked older than she was, and even in costume, you could tell she was beautiful. The high school guys tried to kiss her, and when she refused, they grabbed her. The whole thing happened so fast I just sat there, as though I were the audience and the whole thing was a play. And then it wasn't. I hit one of the guys, and all of my silver bracelets were so heavy he fell backwards. The shock of me smashing one of them gave us time to run. We ran and ran, like we really could get to the moon if we had to. We ran until we turned into smoke; we could float across lawns and drift under windows and doors.

"I can't believe you did that," Jill said when we finally made it home. She had lost her tail and her ears, but her face was shining. "You hit him."

I felt great for days.

We don't do holidays. We go to my grandma Frieda's for Passover, but we skip Chanukah, which my father insists is trivial, and Thanksgiving, which he considers a meaningless ritual. We do, however, spend every Christmas at Margot's house. It's a holiday she feels entitled to celebrate since she was married to Tony Molinaro for all those years. My father never goes to Margot's, and this year Jason wasn't there either. It was just us, and we decorated the tree with all of Tony's mother's beautiful old ornaments. There's an angel that's always been my favorite, fashioned out of silvery glass. When Tony's mother was alive she assured me it would bring good luck to whoever hung it on the tree. Tony's mother always preferred Margot to her own son, and when they broke up she took to her bed and was dead by the following spring.

Even after Margot and Tony divorced, Margot always included her ex-mother-in-law in the festivities. Tony's mother must have been at least ninety. Her hands shook as she held out the angel. "Here's the thing about luck," she told me on her last Christmas. "You don't know if it's good or bad until you have some perspective."

This year we made a toast to the old lady and Margot actually cried. Right as we finished the tree, snow started to fall. We all rushed to the front window to look. It was the kind of snow that you hardly ever see, so heavy and beautiful you fall in love with winter, even though you know you'll have to shovel in the morning.

Margot had made a turkey with stuffing, a noodle kugel, and a white cake topped with coconut that looked like the snow outside. After dinner, she and my mother put on aprons and did the dishes and laughed. I let them listen to Elvis's *Blue Christmas;* I hardly ever saw my mother having a good time, so how could I complain?

In Jill's family Christmas was a big deal, and I knew when I went over to her house in the morning she'd have a dozen great presents to show me and I'd have to try not to be jealous. Jill and I had given each other bottles of White Musk, our favorite scent. I envied Jill just about everything, but I didn't feel jealous right then, listening to Elvis in Margot's house. Truthfully, there was nowhere else I'd rather be. Lucky for us, Margot lived right around the corner from us. Her house was our house, and vice versa, unless my father was at home. Margot and my mother intended to be neighbors forever; they had dozens of plans, but not all of their plans were working out.

I'd overheard my father talking on the phone. He was intending to leave as soon as the weather got better. As soon as he could break the news to us, he'd be gone. He was in a holding pattern, that's what he said, but he wasn't holding on to us, that much was certain. I didn't tell my mother what I'd learned. I didn't tell anyone. I wanted to see Margot and my mother dance in the kitchen when the dishes were done and drying on the rack. I wanted to see them throw their aprons on the floor.

That night, when we walked home, my mother put her arm around me and told me to wish on a star. She still believed in things like that. We stood there in the snow, and try as I might, I didn't see a single star. But I lied. I said that I did, and I wished anyway. We stood there while my mother tried in vain to see that same star. My fingers were freezing, so I put my hands in my pockets. The angel was there. I knew that if I tried to thank Margot, she'd tell me to cut it out, she'd say it was nothing, but it was definitely something to me.

It was late, but we could hear traffic on the Southern State Parkway, even though it was Christmas, and snowing so hard. You had to wonder who all these people in their cars were leaving behind and who they were driving toward, and if they knew that in the distance, the echo of their tires on the asphalt sounded like a river, and that to someone like me, it could seem like the miracle I'd been looking for.

Rose Red

The sky was blue all through June, and if you walked along the streets of our neighborhood you could smell cut grass; you could hear the low humming of bees. School had been out for exactly one week, and my best friend Jill and I were already bored out of our minds. We were twelve, that unpredictable and dangerous age when sampling shades of lipstick and playing with dolls seem equally interesting. We both had the feeling that this summer was our last chance at something, and not knowing quite what it was, we started testing our boundaries. We talked back to our mothers. We streaked our hair with a caustic mixture of peroxide and ammonia. We spoke to strangers and didn't pick up after ourselves. By the end of the month we were climbing out our bedroom windows nearly every night.

We'd meet in Jill's backyard, in the moonlight, beneath a ceiling of distant white stars. We dressed in dark colors, so not even a sleepwalker could spot us. Jill wore black shorts and a black sweatshirt; she hid her pale blond hair under a baseball cap. I always borrowed my brother's old windbreaker and threw on the same pair of black jeans. What we were doing on those midnights, beneath a crooked crab apple tree, was plotting our revenge. It was not simply our neighborhood that we hated, but the entire adult world, which, regretfully, we were soon destined to join. Perhaps this is what made us so giddy and daring, so sure of ourselves, so intense. Ordinarily, we were good girls. We baby-sat, we handed our homework in on time, we washed supper dishes without being asked. But that was all over now. We made a list of the people we hated most: those who had insulted us, or treated us badly, or simply ignored us. Those who were rude or nasty or full of themselves. The names of our neighbors appeared on our list, spelled out in Jill's neat, orderly script.

Mrs. Brandon, who owned the variety store and phoned your mother if you happened to take a pack of gum and forgot to pay, was number one. Then came Mr. DiPietro, who screamed at his wife so loudly you could hear every word when you walked past their open window on warm evenings. There was also Mr. Richie, who had been our fourth-grade teacher, and liked to lock you in the coat closet if you talked out of turn. When our list was complete at last, it was time to take action. We worked at midnight, the hour when every street was silent and every house dark. With our neighbors safely asleep in their beds, we were as free as a nightmare to settle wherever we wished without a witness, except perhaps for prowling cats, let out until morning. We wrote with pieces of coal on Mrs. Brandon's garage door. We emptied an entire container of cottage cheese into Mr. DiPietro's mailbox. When people in the neighborhood began to talk about gremlins, we bit our tongues. We winked at each other and tried not to laugh. Deep inside, we felt the true power of secrecy and revenge.

"Did you hear what somebody did to Mr. Richie?" my brother, Jason, asked me one morning as I was heading over to Jill's and he was dragging our trash out to the curb. "They poured buttermilk into his garbage cans. Pretty cool, huh?"

"Wow," I said.

I didn't have to fake being impressed. I still couldn't believe Jill and I had had the nerve to pull that one off. We'd dumped in two quarts of warm, rancid buttermilk and afterwards we'd run back to her house so fast we both wound up with stitches in our sides. I'd had to kneel down on the ground in order to catch my breath, and Jill had been laughing her head off, and then, from out of nowhere, we'd heard a siren. It sounded as though it was right on our block. Jill and I stared at each other in a complete panic.

"We're insane," Jill said to me in her clear, sweet voice.

She was probably right, and I was about to suggest that we never play these sorts of tricks again, but then the police car turned onto another street, and as soon as the siren faded, so did my resolve. Revenge did that to a person; it caused even the insecure and the meek to take foolhardy chances. After a while it became a way of life: the risks felt as natural as drawing a breath.

The day after the buttermilk incident, Jill and I spent the afternoon at the municipal pool, in awe of our own daring. Everyone was talking about Mr. Richie's garbage cans. It was legend now; it was all over town. Jill and I wore big sunglasses to hide our true natures. Who knew the real us? No one. Who knew what we were capable of? Not a single soul.

We sprawled on beach towels we'd arranged on the cement near the deep end of the pool. I couldn't help but notice how much longer Jill's legs were than mine. This was the summer when she'd suddenly become beautiful; by August people she'd known all her life wouldn't recognize her. *Jill?* they'd say, as though she were a mirage. *Is that you?*

"Maybe we'd better stop while we're ahead." Jill was eating a melting Almond Joy. I, as usual, was on a diet, and had brought carrot sticks along for a snack. I rarely ate anything else and my fingers and toes had a distinctly orange tinge.

"You're kidding, right?" I sounded like a rabbit, but I kept right on crunching. "We're just getting started. And what about Mr. Castle?" I reminded her. "We haven't gotten him yet."

Jill and I both baby-sat for the Castles; they had two cute kids—Amy, who was four, and little Pearl, who was just about the most adorable baby in the world. Twice last month, Mr. Castle had tried some really disgusting things with Jill when he drove her home. Once, he'd insisted she kiss him goodnight, and the other time he did something Jill was too embarrassed to tell me about even though she knew every single detail of my life. I asked and asked; I crossed my heart, vowing never to repeat a word, but still she wouldn't speak.

Well, Jill wasn't baby-sitting for the Castles anymore, and in a show of solidarity, neither was I. Mrs. Castle had called me three times and practically begged, but I told her I had mononucleosis and the prognosis for my recovery wasn't good. To tell you the truth, I felt sorry for Mrs. Castle—she was the type of person who bought extra potato chips and Coke when you baby-sat for her kids, and she always asked what was new in your life, which very few employers bothered to do—but I stuck with my mono story. When Elinor Nagle informed me the Castles had hired her to sit, I told her that Amy was a monster who threw food, and that the baby had diarrhea constantly, and that it was best never to walk barefoot in the Castles' house, since a black widow spider had gotten loose in one of their kitchen cabinets. Later, I heard Elinor never showed up at the Castles', and even though she wasn't a particularly close friend, I was glad she'd had second thoughts.

Taking our revenge on Mr. Castle was different than all the others, and we knew it from the start. We were long past buttermilk and cottage cheese and coal. We were in far more serious territory now. When we met in Jill's backyard we didn't feel giddy anymore; now we were out for real retribution, and there was no backing down. We discussed possibilities we knew we'd never go through with—fires and floods, even vermin. We'd set his garage on fire with kindling and matches. We'd stick the garden hose through his basement window and turn it on full blast. We'd have Monica Greeley's younger brother release the squirrels he trapped down by the creek into Castle's garage. But the truth was, neither of us wanted Mr. Castle's family to suffer, which is why we zeroed in on his car, a new Lincoln he was so crazy about he wouldn't even let Mrs. Castle drive to the store.

Their house was on Maple Avenue, right at the end of the development, next door to the original farmhouse that had been built nearly two hundred years earlier. People we knew avoided this part of town, which made perfect sense. There was nothing beyond this border but a weedy field, and after that a service road which led to the parkway. It was a place that made you feel lonely and disoriented, and that was the way we felt on the night we went to play our last trick. We had appropriated three gallons of paint Jill's father kept stored in their basement. I was only carrying one paint can, but it was heavy; as I walked it bumped against my shins and my knees. Still, I didn't dare complain. After all, Jill was carrying two gallons, and she certainly wasn't whining. She was looking straight ahead, into the dark. The weather was humid and warm; every mosquito in town seemed to have hatched, and each one was hungry for blood. It was the sort of night that feels like a dream, when you're suddenly about to do things you only thought yourself capable of imagining. Before you know it you're inside of something that feels as unavoidable as destiny.

We planned to prepare for our attack behind the hedges that separated the Castle house from the old farmhouse. I had taken a screwdriver out of my brother's toolbox, and had grabbed two pairs of old leather gloves from the coat closet, to ensure that we wouldn't leave fingerprints. Although I hadn't yet informed Jill, I'd already decided this was to be my last revenge. Since we'd begun our paybacks I'd developed a nervous stomach. I'd become afraid of the dark. Even walking on this street in my own neighborhood was giving me the creeps. It seemed as though we could fall off the face of the earth at any time. Just one more step, that's all it would take, and we'd be goners for sure.

"Maybe we should think this over," I whispered to Jill after we reached the Castles'.

"What do you mean?" Jill said. "You were the one who said we should do it."

"I know. But all the other stuff was fooling around. This could be considered a felony or something. I think I changed my mind."

"Well, I haven't," Jill said.

I had always believed that of the two of us I was the leader. Now, I wasn't so sure.

"What if damaging a motor vehicle is a federal offense?" I asked. "We could go to jail."

If Jill had argued or called me a big baby, maybe I would have turned and walked home. But instead, she started to cry. She stood there, beside the hedges, all dressed in black, and she lowered her head so I couldn't see, but I knew anyway. Her shoulders always shook like that whenever she cried.

"Oh, what the hell." I gave in. "He deserves it."

We crept through a hole in the hedges in complete and utter silence. We were barely breathing, and we were thinking even less. We set the paint cans down, but before we went farther we realized something was different on this side of the hedges. We breathed deeply, and deeper still. The air was amazingly sweet, and when we crept forward we saw the reason why. The old farmhouse was covered with roses, little red roses that were all opening on this night. There were so many blossoms they covered the peeling clapboards; vines twisted over the roof, making it impossible to tell how many shingles had been blown away by last winter's storms.

"Have you ever seen anything like this?" I asked Jill, but she wasn't listening. She had already pulled on her black leather gloves; now she handed me the other pair.

"Hurry up," she told me. "Let's get the tops off the paint cans."

I'd been past this old house a thousand times and never

noticed roses before. Could it be that they bloomed only at this hour, or on this day? Could it be I'd never bothered to look? I just had to have one of those roses. I had to have proof that something like this could grow in our town.

"I'll be right back," I whispered to Jill, and before she could react I went right up to the house. I had never seen anything as lovely. It was the sort of beauty you feel so deeply it becomes contagious and somehow makes you beautiful too. I was so involved with looking at the roses that I didn't even realize someone was out on the front porch until it was too late for me to run. I knew it was Mrs. Dennison, even though I'd never seen her before. People in town said she was a hundred; she'd grown up in this house and her family had owned the potato farm that had been chopped into tiny lots when the land was first developed. Mrs. Dennison was wacko, that's what I'd heard. She kept a shotgun in her parlor; she hated people. If you dared to walk across her front lawn, you'd better beware.

"I wasn't doing anything," I said as soon as I saw Mrs. Dennison, though, certainly, I looked guilty as sin.

"Well, go on, take it," she said to me.

"Take what?" I said, but I could see right then that Mrs. Dennison wasn't easy to fool.

"Go on," she told me. She nodded at the roses.

"All right. Fine." I took a flower from the branch closest to me.

"Do you have those gloves on for a reason?" Mrs. Dennison asked.

I could have lied to her then, but I didn't. It wouldn't

have done any good, I could see that. One thing people didn't bother to report about Mrs. Dennison was how smart she was, a hundred years old or not.

"If I told you why I had these gloves on, you'd be a coconspirator, so I'd better not say any more."

"Don't say another word." Mrs. Dennison seemed to understand.

Jill was signaling to me like crazy.

"Your friend's upset." Mrs. Dennison could judge things in an instant, that much was clear.

"She's got her reasons," I said.

"I planted these roses when I was your age," Mrs. Dennison told me. "And look at them now."

"Pretty impressive. Actually, they're amazing."

By then I had tears in my eyes. Sometimes, the world cracks open to reveal itself to you in a single instant. Standing there in the dark, humid night, I realized there was no turning back. We could try to stop it, we could drag our feet, but we were going forward, no matter what. When Mrs. Dennison went inside, I brought the rose with me and walked back to where Jill was crouched in the dark.

"Well, that's the end of this plan." Jill's voice sounded shaky, as if she were exhausted.

"Why?" It was the oddest thing how the scent of roses stayed with you.

"Because she'll turn us in. She can identify us."

"She won't," I said.

"You can't know that," Jill insisted.

But some things you do know, you know them for sure. For instance, I was certain that when I ran into the Castles' driveway and lifted the can, white paint would spread out in pools on the roof of that Lincoln, then spill down over the hood. It was oil paint, so white it was hypnotic, almost like watching the stars. I might have stood beside the car forever if Jill hadn't grabbed my arm. As we ran we left footprints of paint on the asphalt, but Jill was clearheaded; she made sure we stopped and took off our shoes before we made too much of a trail.

Jill had also thought to grab the paint cans and the screwdriver; by the time the police were called the next morning, there wasn't any evidence left. Nearly everyone in the neighborhood was questioned, but nobody knew a thing. Two cats were found with oily white feet, and a rose dipped in paint was discovered at the corner of Maple Avenue; beyond that there wasn't a clue. I still wonder what Mrs. Dennison told the police. Sometimes I think she sleepwalked out to her porch that night, and believed our conversation to be a dream, although when I went out to see her the following Friday, she knew exactly who I was.

At any rate, the police never found out who ruined Mr. Castle's Lincoln. No further information was ever unearthed, in spite of Mr. Castle's offer of a five-hundred-dollar reward for any tips leading to an arrest. Sometimes, for no reason at all, Jill laughs out loud, and I always think she's remembering that night we attacked Mr. Castle's car. But you never can tell. You can only know a friend so well, after all. When you come right down to it, even your best friend is a puzzle. Jill, for instance, is convinced that I still go to visit Mrs. Dennison because I'm afraid she'll turn us in, but that isn't the reason. I go to sit on the porch, that's all. I go to hear how it used to be in our neighborhood when there wasn't another house for miles around, how twilight came so slowly then, how the roses bloomed all summer long.

Flight

Eugene Kessler was supposed to be my brother's best friend, but he and I actually had a lot more in common. It wasn't so much that Eugene and I liked each other, or that there was any possibility of romance between us. It was more that we both despised Franconia, the suburb where we were doomed to live. In Franconia, no one's imagination was working overtime, that much was evident from the moment you first walked through town, where you could find the Franconia High School, the Franconia Mall, the Franconia Diner, and, for special occasions—

proms, for instance, or extramarital trysts—the Franconia Steak House, which Eugene and I called Marie's, not only because Marie Fortuna's husband caught her there, eating antipasto with her boyfriend, who happened to be the soccer coach at the high school, but because we couldn't stand to hear the word Franconia used one more time.

Eugene and I were in business together, earning money for our escape from town by selling term papers, and June was our busiest time of the year. By the end of the month, however, we were no longer doing our best work. The pressure was on, the stupid among us had panicked, and I was writing all night. In part, I kept odd hours because my brother strongly disapproved of our venture, and Jason was so honest and good that a single look from him could make a person feel sordid and corrupt. But the real reason I was writing three or more papers at a time was that Eugene was in charge of the division of labor, and he'd divided it so that two thirds of the labor was mine. After all, he had started the business, so it was only fair that he administered everything, including our finances, which were kept in a joint savings account. Or at least, this was Eugene's line every time I complained. And when I really considered my situation, it wasn't so difficult to accept the deal he offered and keep my mouth shut. In August, Eugene would be leaving—he and my brother had done what no one in our town had ever managed before and had both gotten into Harvard—at which point the business would be all mine.

So I kept cranking out term papers. I went through the great religions of the world, then turned to literature—Shakespeare's comedies for the juniors, tragedies for the seniors. I wrote dream journals and essays about my various families, some so moving I brought myself to tears. At least, writing these papers kept my mind off the heat, which was nearly unbearable that June. I had a lot not to think about back then, including the horrible noise the cicadas made all day and night, an echo that could lead you to believe little bombs were going off on your neighbors' front lawns. I certainly didn't want to dwell on the fact that I'd probably ruined my hair for good. I had dyed it black and cut the front much too short, using a dull nail scissors, so that I now looked as though I were in a constant state of shock. Well, maybe I was, and maybe I had good reason to be. Not long ago my father had moved out and now my mother barely left her room. Even our dog, a Labrador retriever known to do little but sleep, had attacked Mrs. Fisher's cat across the street and now, instead of roaming the neighborhood, he was chained up in our yard, eating cicadas, making himself sick.

Through it all, the heat just kept getting worse. At school, people fainted during homeroom. There were fights in the parking lot of the Franconia Mall, real fights that were bloody and unforgiving and hot. After a while, all anyone could hear were those horrible cicadas and the whirring of air conditioners. It got so that I hated everyone—not Jason of course, who was too pure to hate, just everyone else who lived and breathed inside the Franconia town limits.

The only one who seemed to understand me at that point in time was Eugene Kessler, and this notion was just about as scary as any I'd ever had. On truly hot nights, when the air was so humid and thick it was a triumph to draw a deep breath, I would sometimes see Eugene out in his yard. Somehow, I knew how alone he felt, and it gave me the shivers to think that alienation could be a shared experience. Eugene had found a great horned owl at a rest area on the parkway two summers earlier. Now, on nights when everyone else was at home with the air conditioner turned on high, Eugene would let the owl fly free. He'd been informed by a lieutenant down at the police department that he'd better keep the owl caged at all times, because of an incident involving a toy poodle that had been carried off, but Eugene had his own view of natural selection. He figured that the Yorkie who lived on the corner, and the Chihuahua who snarled from behind a fence over on Maple, had better run for cover when they spied the owl's shadow above them. In Eugene's opinion, their fate was in their own paws.

Jason was different. He wasn't like Eugene, and he certainly wasn't like me. He always played by the rules. My brother was so serious and straightlaced that teenage girls were constantly after him. Several had spent all year attempting to seduce him, but Jason had other things on his mind. He'd devoted every free minute to his senior science thesis. Twenty hamsters were kept in cages in his bedroom.

Ten had been given a balanced diet of seeds and grains, but the other ten had eaten nothing but Twinkies. My brother hoped to finish his research before leaving for college, although to me it already seemed obvious that the Twinkie ten were not only fatter but far more intelligent. As soon as they heard my brother's bedroom door open, they ran to their feeding stations, while the grain and nut hamsters just went on running on their wheels, making the same hopeless circles they spun every night.

Maybe Jason would have finished his research if Eugene had remembered to write Joey Jergens's history paper, but Eugene was too busy planning his future, plotting his imminent escape, to pay much attention to our schedule. Eugene had missed the delivery date and Joey was outraged when he called me. I had to soothe him with promises of ten pages on the Salem witch trials by eight the following morning.

"Don't be mad," Eugene said as soon as he saw me the next day.

We were in the field behind the high school and Joey was headed straight for us. Of course, I refused to speak to Eugene. I had slept for two hours. I was in no mood for this.

"I'll do the *Romeo and Juliet* for Sue Greco," Eugene vowed. He knew I dreaded Shakespeare papers, and had one of my own past due. "The Industrial Revolution for Horowitz?" Eugene whispered. "Consider it done."

By now, Joey Jergens was upon us. "Got my paper?"

Joey was not a conversationalist, but it was enough that he had taken fifteen dollars out of his jeans pocket. I started to hand over the opus I'd written, but Eugene grabbed for it. "Let me check for typos," he said.

"No way," I said. "Who sat up all night with this thing? This paper's mine."

"Be careful with that," Joey Jergens warned me, and maybe I was clutching on too tightly. But Eugene was trying to pry my hard work away, and I wouldn't let him, and that was how Mr. Prospero, the vice principal, found us, struggling over a report neither of us cared about, enmeshed in a battle that would only cause us grief.

By nine-fifteen we were all suspended. Joey Jergens had been expecting to go to summer school, so it didn't matter much to him, but now Eugene wouldn't graduate. Maybe he stood there for a while, staring at the high school, and maybe he didn't. I don't know. I immediately headed for home. I was thinking about myself and no one else. I had just lost the summer, after all. Other people would be having a life, I'd be reading *Romeo and Juliet* in a classroom hot enough to bake bread on the desks.

Naturally, my brother blamed me for everything. He didn't care that Eugene had started the business and had practically drafted me.

"He can still go to Cambridge with you," I told my brother, even though I knew it wasn't true. You couldn't enroll for more than two classes in the summer, and Eugene would be missing four credits.

My brother phoned Eugene, ready to let him have it for throwing his future away for fifteen lousy dollars, but when Jason came back into the living room he didn't seem mad anymore. Eugene had already been to the bank and withdrawn our entire joint savings. Then he'd gone home and left a note for his mother in which he swore he would pay me back someday, although I certainly wasn't about to hold my breath. Eugene had also informed his mother that he was buying a plane ticket and by the time she read his note he'd already be on his way to San Francisco. Maybe I should have been angry about working all year for nothing, but I wasn't. I went over and let Mrs. Kessler tell me about the way Eugene had taught himself to read the dictionary when he was two and a half, even though I'd heard the story about a million times before. Mrs. Kessler had a weird look on her face, and it made me think of my mother, just after my father had left her. It made me think that summer would never be the same, not now and not ever.

I guess deep inside I did believe everything that had happened was my fault. I must have, because sometime between the moment when I got to the Kesslers' and the moment when I left, I told Eugene's mother I'd be glad to take care of the owl until Eugene returned. Of course, Mrs. Kessler was delighted to get rid of the owl. She got down on her knees and helped me coax it into its cage. I walked home carefully, trying not to jostle the owl, but as soon as I set the cage down on our living room floor, I realized my mistake. Somehow, the owl looked much bigger in our house. Its feet were as big as our Labrador retriever's. I couldn't even stand to be in the same room as Eugene's horrible pet. I went to the kitchen and telephoned everyone I knew to announce my suspension from school, but it wasn't the same as talking to Eugene. Still, I talked for a long time, long enough so that Jason was the one who discovered that the owl had killed every one of his hamsters. Either the cage had been left open or the owl knew some tricks I wasn't aware of. Frankly, its method of escape didn't matter. By the time Jason walked into his bedroom, the owl was sitting on the air conditioner, distressed and thwarted, its feathers ruffled; although it had managed to kill all the hamsters, it still couldn't get to them through the meshing of their cages.

My brother had hoped to finish his experiment before leaving for college; now he didn't have to worry. It was over. If the owl hadn't belonged to Eugene, I think Jason would have killed it. Instead, he went out and bought six live chicks at the pet store. But the owl wouldn't eat. We watched over it for days and then weeks, but the owl never really recovered. Maybe the heat was what caused its feathers to drop out, one by one, as it perched on the air conditioner. Or maybe it was only longing for someone who wasn't afraid to let it fly above the poplars and crab apples, searching backyards, a streak of lightning in our dark sky.

Gretel

It was a bad summer, and we all knew it. We liked to phrase it that way, as if what was happening was an aberration—a single season of pain and doubt—instead of all-out informing people that our lives were falling apart, plain and simple as pie. I knew too much for someone who was fifteen, and with the way my luck was running, I'd probably soon know more. I was no longer one of those human beings who blithely assume that everything can't go wrong at the same time. Even my best friend Jill, who was without a doubt the most cheerful person I'd ever met, shook her head and said "Wow" whenever I told her what was going on in our family. She sat cross-legged on my bed, obsessively eating M&M's, and informed me that in light of my family's bad luck it was only natural for me to experience a crisis of confidence. But Jill was good-natured and liked to see the best in every situation. Frankly, I didn't see the difference between a crisis of confidence and a nervous breakdown.

At least I was in the right place. People in our town had nervous breakdowns all the time. It was one of Franconia's claims to fame. The luncheonette was a regular hotbed of lunatics. Not that you could tell by looking at them. They appeared normal enough at first glance, but if you kept on looking you'd see that the woman who had ordered black coffee was crying hot tears into her cup, and the man beside her, who liked his eggs sunny-side up, was talking to himself, having a grand old conversation with the person he most respected. Even Jill's mom, who was the head of the PTA and made the best chocolate chip cookies in town, had received shock treatments last fall, and although she was nowhere as depressed as she'd been before, her baking was the victim of her new emotional state; it was all bland and soapy now, not worth the calories or the time it took to chew.

My mother had always been an eyewitness to other people's problems, yet refused to have any of her own. She was smart and funny; she told good jokes and smoked Salem cigarettes and continued to believe in true love even though she had married my father, who could put anyone through a crisis of confidence.

After he left, my father became involved with a woman named Thea, whom he married on the Fourth of July. Anyone needing to know the facts about the wedding had better ask someone else, since I was not invited. I didn't even find out about it until a week after it happened, when my brother came over to Jill's house, something he never did. Jason was going off to college in the fall, or at least that had been the plan, but lately he didn't seem to be going anywhere fast. The week after his best friend, my former business partner, Eugene, had run off to California, Jason had gotten himself a job at the Food Star, in the deli department, and something had shifted. He was starting to seem comfortable in the deli. He was even dating a girl who worked in fruits and vegetables—Terry LoPacca, who wore huge hoop earrings and was so inarticulate she merely smiled if you asked her a question. To be honest, Jason wouldn't have looked at Terry when he was still in school. He probably didn't even know she was alive until he found her beside the lemons and the limes, her pretty face upturned, alight with her glorious smile.

When my brother came to get me at Jill's he didn't even look like himself. Who was he? That's what I wanted to know. What was happening to our family, anyway? Jason had won every science prize at school and had gotten early admission to Harvard, but now he wore an old, grungy T-shirt and was smoking a Salem that he'd swiped from my mother; he had smoked that cigarette right down to the filter, and he wasn't done with it yet. I think he had stopped sleeping, because his face, which was usually open and sweet, had a twisted look. Even Jill, Miss I-See-the-Silver-Lining, could detect the toll our family's bad fortune had taken on Jason.

"Wow," she said when she saw him coming, cutting across the Fishers' yard, completely unaware that he was trampling the impatiens and the dahlias. "He looks awful," she sighed in her sunny little voice, which made everything seem even more hopeless than it was.

The worst thing, of course, was that our mother was sick. She'd been diagnosed in May, but she'd kept her illness from us. At first we thought she was sleeping all the time because she was depressed that our father had taken up with Thea, who, naturally, was ten years younger than my mother, just to add insult to the injury of their affair. My mother, you understand, was not a person who slept much under normal circumstances. Ordinarily, she'd still be talking to her friends on the telephone at midnight, or trying out a new recipe; at the oddest hours imaginable you'd find her repainting the kitchen tiger-lily orange or pale green. Her eyes were fiery and black and she talked back to the TV. *Big shot,* she'd say to the actors who treated their women all wrong. *Get a life,* she'd cry to any woman who dissolved in a heap of makeup and tears. But now things had changed. She stayed in bed all afternoon, and she'd lost a lot of weight; late at night, when she thought I was asleep, I could hear her crying.

It was Jill's mom who told me that my mother had cancer. I was over for dinner and Mrs. Harrington took me into their backyard and put her hands on my shoulders as we stood beside the jungle gym we were all too old for, and then she told me. Right there and for my own good. That's the way we always found out things about our own family, in a roundabout fashion that made us feel even sadder than we would have if we'd known the truth straight out. Now, in July, when the heat was unbearable and the cicadas sang a maddened song all day long, my brother nodded to me in the manner he'd recently affected, as if there was nothing he cared about in the whole wide world.

We didn't talk until we'd left Jill's house and were headed for home. All around us the asphalt was melting, and we were most likely thinking the same thing—that good old Eugene Kessler, who had run away in June, was surely in a much, much better place than we were right now.

"They got married," my brother told me. He had that look on his face, the twisted one.

I had no idea who he was referring to, but I kept my mouth shut until I figured out he was talking about my father and Thea. I was wearing a lot of mascara in those days, so it often seemed that I was tearful, even when I was not.

"Cut it out," my brother said to me in a mean voice. He never used to sound that way, but I had to face it. He sounded like that now.

"Cut what out?" I said. I suppose he thought I was crying, which I absolutely was not. "Does Mom know?" I asked when our house came into sight. It was just like every other house on the street, but for some reason it looked more decrepit than all the rest. At least to me.

I guess it was no longer possible for my brother to answer a direct question. "They're picking us up at six," he told me, and he slammed through the front door.

Our house was dark in the summer, because of the two cypresses my father had planted in the front yard, but it was still stuffy and hot. I went to the doorway of my mother's bedroom. She was under her quilt in spite of the heat, and I couldn't tell if she was sleeping or not.

"I hear the stinker is coming to see you," she said.

Since she was awake I went to sit on the edge of the bed. She had cups of water and orange juice on her night table, but she didn't care; her throat was too raw to swallow anything. Her eyes were more fevered than ever. Sometimes it seemed as if she could see everything, as if she could look directly into your soul.

"If he takes you to a restaurant, order the most expensive thing on the menu," my mother instructed. "It doesn't matter if you eat it or not. Have three appetizers. Start with shrimp cocktail."

We laughed over that, since my father hated to spend money. He also hated unkempt girls, he thought they were a terrible disgrace, so I put on my oldest jeans and a shirt that was torn and stained. My hair was growing out from a horrible haircut I'd given myself only a few weeks earlier. I looked pretty much the way I felt, and I didn't bother to talk when Jason came out to wait with me on the stoop.

At six-fifteen my father's car pulled up to the curb. That awful Thea was behind the wheel. We'd met her a couple of times, but hadn't paid much attention. Now, as she honked the horn, I realized she was my mother's exact opposite—self-centered and ravenous. That was the thing about my mother—there was hardly anything she'd ever wanted for herself. She'd had her eye on a dining room set once, and she never even got to have that.

"Hurry up," Thea called to us. "We'll be late."

It turned out my father was coming directly from work and would meet us at the restaurant, Luarano's over in Rose Village, an expensive place a few towns past ours that I'd never been to before, although I was pretty certain they'd have shrimp cocktail. If I was lucky, they'd have oysters too.

Thea tore through our neighborhood as if running over some kid playing kickball would be a far better option than keeping my father waiting at a restaurant. The windows were open and when the car turned onto the parkway the air was like a rocket of pure heat blasting right through us.

Thea was talking about what a great place we were going to for dinner, and how they liked people to dress nicely, which of course was a dig at me, not that I cared about her sense of style. Then she started in on her real agenda—how the house she and my father had recently bought might look big, but it was really just right for two people. I guess she wanted to squelch any ideas we might have about moving in with them, although frankly we would have preferred to nest with spiders. I could see Jason's profile, and he looked absolutely blank. He was doing that lately. You could knock and knock, but he wouldn't let you in. During a period of three months he'd gone from someone who had always planned his career at Harvard to a deli boy who appeared to have undergone a lobotomy.

Thea was driving much too fast and talking even faster. I guess she was telling us the score, in her sly, understated manner, informing us that we were second-class citizens, as if we didn't already know that. If my mother had been one of the passengers, she would have demanded Thea pull over. Once, when we were little, my mother went right up to our bus driver who'd been speeding all the way to Atlantic City, and smacked him. Some of the other passengers actually applauded, and you can bet the driver slowed down after that.

Thea finally turned off the parkway, but she kept right on speeding. Every minute she was spending with us was probably killing her, so she took the shortcut through the forest. It was a creepy stretch where the county police sometimes trained recruits; some people said that beneath the ivy and the wild grass, there were sinkholes that could suck you right into the ground if you wandered off in the wrong direction.

Though it was dark in the woods, Thea didn't bother to switch on her fog lights. She was too busy talking about the furniture she'd just picked out. That's when I started to take things out of her purse. It had been sitting there beside me on the back seat all this time, a fat leather bag with gold clasps and a nasty disposition. The first thing I got was her wallet, crammed with credit cards. I slipped them out the open window, one by one, then went on to the cash. It felt so wonderful to release all those tens and twenties into the wind; I couldn't have felt any better if I'd been freeing caged parakeets to nest among tropical palms. I should have kept it to that, nice flat items like money and credit cards, but instead I went on to harder stuff: vials of prescriptions, silver tubes of lipstick, brushes, tortoiseshell combs, opal earrings in a velvet box.

Maybe Thea caught sight of what I was doing, or maybe she looked in her rearview mirror and spied her belongings scattered across the road. There was her chiffon scarf, caught in the bushes. There were her sunglasses, floating in the drainage ditch. She pulled the car over so fast our heads snapped back. We probably would have had just cause to call a personal injury lawyer and claim whiplash, but Thea wasn't the type to give you time to consider your options.

"Your father is right," she said to me. She formed her words carefully, the way people do when they want to hurt you. "You are a little bitch."

Our mother always told us that people will surely reveal what they're made of, if you only give them the chance. What's deep inside always surfaces, no matter how hidden.

"Wait a minute," Jason said to our new stepmother. "You can't talk to my sister like that."

But the truth was, she could. She told us to get out and get out fast. She was already putting the car into gear.

"Here?" Jason said. "You'd just leave us?"

He had a funny look on his face, and for a moment it seemed as if he might actually hit Thea, simply reach over and slap her. But instead, he slammed the door open and got out. I followed just in time; Thea stepped on the gas before I could close the door, and as the car took off down the road the door flapped open and shut, like a broken wing.

"You are a moron," my brother told me as the car exhaust rose above us in thick black clouds.

I thought about how people threw each other away, as if they were tissues or trash. I thought about my mother, asleep beneath her quilt on this hot summer evening, and the way things moved away from you if you weren't careful, if you didn't hold on tight.

"Don't worry," I told my brother. "I know the way home."

The sky was the color of ashes and we both studied it carefully for some sort of sign. Behind us was a ribbon of road and woods so thick you'd need an ax to find your way. It was only dinnertime, but it felt later.

"Face it," my brother finally said to me. "We're lost."

Tell the Truth

Our dog, Revolver, ran away and I can't say that I blame him. He was a cat chaser and I guess he had to pay, because when my mother received her twenty-first complaint about his activities she had my brother tie the dog up to the cherry tree, which was the tallest, sturdiest thing in our yard. All the same, Revolver was so exuberant and single-minded, in the way of Labrador retrievers, and so intent on freedom, that the kids in the neighborhood began to take bets, first on whether or not Revolver would manage to get away; then, as the summer wore on, hotter and hotter still, until the sky was perfectly flat and white, wages were laid on the exact hour and day of his escape.

"Do you think he's strong enough to pull the tree out of the ground?" my best friend Jill wanted to know. We were out beneath the cherry tree, sneaking cigarettes, on a morning when the heat was so dense that smoke refused to rise.

"Physically impossible," I said, but it was just a guess. Who can gauge strength under pressure? What about those women who lifted two-thousand-pound Oldsmobiles off the ground in order to rescue their babies? What about men who walked over burning-hot coals?

My mother had been sick all summer and Jill's mother had been ill too, although what Mrs. Harrington had was all in her mind. Jill's father insisted the problem was nothing more than exhaustion, but it was another nervous breakdown, and they obviously did something major while she was away at the hospital, because this time when she came home, Mrs. Harrington wasn't speaking. Not one word.

"I think of it this way," Jill had told me, about her mother's current state. "One less person to boss me around."

All the same, it was creepy over at Jill's house. You'd go into the kitchen and rifle through the fridge looking for a snack, thinking you were alone; then you'd turn and there Mrs. Harrington would be, watching you, all quiet and white, a ghost in the corner, a person who'd had a piece removed from her soul.

Jill and I both avoided going home. We stuck to street corners and backyards. Early in the morning we'd sit beneath the cherry tree and plan our day; then we'd return at twilight. Revolver was always there, tied up and panting, studying us with his big brown eyes, as if he understood us completely. There are times when certain people can't seem to avoid pain; it's everywhere you go, it sticks like glue, and that was what seemed to happen to me and to Jill. It may have been our age, or our inclination, but somehow we'd gotten stuck in the middle of sorrow, and the dog was right there with us, tied by his thick rope, the prisoner of a twenty-foot radius. Ordinarily, Revolver was a great runner; he put his whole heart into it, for better or for worse. Once, when I was walking him, he'd spied a squirrel, and he'd just taken off, pulling me so hard I'd fallen in the street and broken my wrist. But I didn't hold it against him. It was inhuman to keep an animal like Revolver tied up, or maybe it was all too human to be so cruel.

"This is a crime against nature," I declared as I stroked Revolver's big, square head.

"Oh, yeah?" Jill said. "What isn't?"

It was the summer when Jill first became cynical. Before that, before all the sickness and heat, she was the sweetest girl you'd ever met. But lately, she saw the dark underside of everything. She even insisted that my brother, who had always been close to perfect, would come to no good. Everything was bad news, in Jill's opinion. Everything was a game you couldn't win.

It certainly looked that way for Revolver; all he could do was stare at the birds on the lawn, sparrows and wrens he knew he'd never catch. My father had bought him years ago, assuming his dog would be a perfect companion, silent and strong and obedient, everything his family was not. But as it turned out, my father couldn't get Revolver to behave. The dog always jumped on him as soon as he walked through the door, then would refuse to sit or stay. Still, when my father moved out, Revolver howled all night, a terrible sound we'd never heard before, the kind of noise you wouldn't dream a dog could make. That was when he started chasing cats, although he never once killed any he managed to snag. He just kept them between his front paws and chewed the fur along their spines, which was fine until Mrs. Raymond's old Persian died of fright while in Revolver's grasp. Mrs. Raymond's had been the twenty-first complaint, the call which had sealed our dog's fate, and now she looked out her window through a pair of binoculars each day, just to make sure Revolver was still tied up tight.

"Bitch," Jill said to Mrs. Raymond, over the fences and across the yards.

On this morning it was so hot that the sky had begun to rumble, as if ready to explode. There was a fly on the edge of Revolver's nose, but he didn't move. He looked like the animals you see in the worst zoos: monkeys who gaze at you with vacant eyes, gazelles who can no longer run, birds in cages, lions who refuse to roar.

All that day I thought about the fly on Revolver's nose. Jill and I went swimming in her cousin Marianne's backyard pool even though Marianne herself refused to join in because of the distant thunder.

"You'll get hit by lightning if there's a storm," she warned us.

"Good," we told her as we floated on our backs, hair trailing behind us like seaweed. "We'd be glad if we were."

That night the sky kept on rumbling, and I couldn't sleep. It was past midnight when I went into the yard, so dark it was impossible to see Revolver's black coat against the black night. But I could hear the thump of his tail as I approached. I could feel him, curled up at the base of the tree. Your eyes can get used to shadows, quicker than you'd think. I carefully sawed through the rope with a steak knife; it was a job well done, but after that I always knew which knife it was: the dull one. The one that could barely cut through butter.

Revolver came up to me as soon as he was free, not in the way he usually did, leaping, being crazy. He just leaned against my legs. His weight against me felt good, but I moved away and slipped off his collar.

"Go on," I said.

The gate was open.

"Go," I told him, and for once he actually listened. Revolver disappeared into the shadows. I could hear him though, running across the dry grass. I stood there listening, and then I went back inside.

After I'd gotten into bed, the thunder came closer. Sometime in the night, while we all slept, the cherry tree was uprooted. My brother insisted it had been hit by lightning, but my mother believed the damage had been caused by the wind, which had come up before dawn to shake all the birds' nests from the trees and topple huge willows and the tallest poplars. In the morning, my mother phoned the pound, and the police, and even our vet. Each one gave her the same advice: Wait and your dog will show up. But I knew he wouldn't. I didn't bother to go along with Jason and my mother when they drove slowly through our rain-soaked neighborhood, hopefully whistling and scanning the streets. I didn't bother to inform them otherwise when they insisted that Revolver would still be in the backyard if not for that horrible storm.

It rained all that next day, a drenching rain that filled gutters and left floods in people's basements. Little frogs appeared on front lawns and porches. I threw on my mother's old raincoat, grabbed a pair of fishing boots that my father had left behind, and still managed to get soaked as I ran to Jill's house. The lawns were all squelchy and filled with worms. The air was white and hot and wet. I let myself into Jill's house by the side door, the way I always did, but Jill wasn't there. You can tell when a house is empty; there's a sound it has, an echo that's unmistakable, or so I then thought. I was certain the Harringtons had all gone off for the day, to Jill's grandmother's, or to her cousin Marianne's. I gazed at the parakeet that was kept in a cage in the kitchen; I leafed through the calendar on the wall and took a mint from the candy dish. It wasn't until I went to the cupboard for a glass that I realized Mrs. Harrington was there. I may have gasped; I may have grabbed at my chest. I know for a fact that I told myself I'd better breathe evenly, because if I didn't, I'd embarrass myself even further and faint.

"You scared me," I said, as if that weren't completely obvious. I had already backed up, toward the door. In those days, Mrs. Harrington seemed made out of vapor, rather than flesh and blood. Jill had reported that her mother ate only pink grapefruit and melba toast. She drank only water. She hardly slept at all.

"Well, I'd better go," I added casually, still desperate to get out of there. "My dog ran away last night, so I should probably go look for him."

"I saw him," Mrs. Harrington said.

I wasn't certain if she'd really spoken, or if I'd imagined it. Her words seemed made out of vapor as well, smoky little things you had to bend close to decipher. Even if she was Jill's mother and I'd known her forever, she was spooky.

"I don't think so," I told her. "He ran away."

"He was here," she insisted. "On my lawn." She sounded a little panicky. "I know it for a fact. He was right here."

"Okay," I said. After all, I was equally panicked, but I knew that with adults it was always best to agree. Humor them, that's what Jill and I had decided, and they'll leave you alone. "I'll check your lawn first."

I let the door slam behind me and started running, in spite of the heavy fishing boots I was wearing, in spite of the rain. I didn't stop when I reached my house. I kept right on going, past the street corners where Jill and I had spent most of our summer, past the high school, where classes would be starting in only a few weeks.

Behind the school there was a creek that was usually nothing more than a dried-out sandy bed. But on this day, it was nearly a river. All the gutters led here, all the flooded streets emptied into this one swollen conduit. Today, the water would rise higher than it ever had before. It would run through the tunnels, it would go on and on, and for some reason, that made me feel better than I had in a very long time.

All the rest of that summer, there were reports of our dog being sighted. People swore he was the reason there were so many overturned garbage cans in the neighborhood; they blamed him when their cats refused to go out at night and when their grass was torn up. The owner of the deli entertained his customers with stories of a black dog who waited for the bakery truck in the morning to beg for doughnuts. The pizza guy would tell anyone willing to listen that a dog often sneaked into his kitchen to steal mozzarella and sausage. Mrs. Raymond insisted that she frequently saw the shadow of a huge dog cross her lawn, and she spoke with such certainty that even my brother grew to believe her and took to leaving bowls of kibble out on the sidewalk. By then Mrs. Harrington had begun to talk as if she hadn't had a lapse of any sort, but she never once mentioned seeing our dog. Occasionally, I saw her looking out the window, surveying her own front lawn, but I was fairly certain that she was as convinced as I was. That dog was gone.

How to Talk to the Dead

Two days after Gretel Samuelson's grandmother moved in with them, Gretel discovered her down on her knees in the kitchen, looking up past the chandelier, as though she could see through the ceiling, right into heaven. To get a true cleanliness fanatic like Grandma Frieda onto a floor which hadn't been mopped for a month was some sort of inverted miracle in itself. Usually, Frieda would have attacked the sticky traces of jelly and tomato sauce with Lestoil and a scrub brush. Now, she didn't even seem to notice the dirt. Right away Gretel thought, *Heart attack*. She thought, *Stroke*. She thought, *I really cannot go through any more sorrow.*

The truth was, Gretel had become cynical and snappish. Her family had fallen apart, and Gretel had too. She'd started to chew her cuticles until they bled. She smoked too much; she was unable to sleep. She had come to believe there were little stones in her veins where the blood used to be, hard, cold things that rattled and rolled whenever any real emotion was called for.

On the day when her grandmother spoke to heaven, Gretel had been wasting time as usual, sneaking cigarettes out behind a large catalpa tree and feeling sorrier for herself than any person has a right to. As soon as she walked through the back door to find her eighty-four-year-old grandmother kneeling on the linoleum, Gretel knew something was seriously wrong. She could feel the stones inside her hit against each other.

"Grandma?" Gretel said.

Frieda's mouth was moving a mile a minute, but no sound escaped. This was not a woman who wished to engage in idle conversation. All the same, Gretel took a step closer. "Are you trying to say something?" she asked.

Gretel's grandmother waved one hand in the air and didn't bother to answer. She loved her granddaughter dearly, but Frieda did not like to be interrupted, especially while she was making a deal with the powers that be. This was the sort of bargain you make only once in a lifetime. The deal was simple and pulled no punches; there were no fancy addenda, no clauses, no strings of any kind. All

Frieda was asking for was her daughter's life in exchange for her own. Her daughter, Frances, was supposedly cancer-free since her last operation, but Frieda never had trusted doctors. You wanted something done, you had to do it yourself.

Frieda got up off her knees, refusing her granddaughter's offer of help. Immediately, she began to get ready to die. First, she reached into her pocket and pulled out a twenty.

"Get a pizza," she told her granddaughter, a nice girl in spite of her gloomy attitude. "Bring me the change."

"You get sick when you eat pizza," Gretel reminded her grandmother.

"Watch and see." Frieda wagged a finger as if to suggest that Gretel still had a whole lot to learn.

Gretel went to her mother's bedroom and knocked on the door. They'd moved the TV inside and Frances was sitting up in bed, watching a movie about true love and crying. Frankly, Frances had a lot to cry about. Whenever she thought about her ex-husband, she was brought to tears. She had even gone to a hypnotist in Brooklyn to remove his betrayal from her mind, but by the time she was walking back to her parked car, she was already imagining her ex and his new wife picking out furniture for their house.

Franny, her ex had always said with a sigh when she was the one who wanted anything. *You know we can't afford that.*

But, as it turned out, he could afford plenty, although that didn't change the fact that there still wasn't a decent piece of furniture in the house he'd left behind. Frances knew it was all worthless; on the day Sam left she'd called the Salvation Army, hoping to get rid of everything they had owned together, but the pickup guys had refused to accept the living room suite. Too worn, they'd said. Too ratty and beat-up.

"Grandma wants me to get her a pizza." Gretel threw herself down across the foot of her mother's bed. "I think she's lost her marbles."

"Is she cleaning?" Usually, the house was enough of a mess to keep Frieda busy and out of everyone's hair.

"Nope. She's not even vacuuming. She's just talking to the ceiling and asking for pizza."

Frances took a sip of water and considered. She'd lost weight, and her right side, where they'd operated, still felt weak. In the last few months, she'd had a lot of time to consider the state of mankind, and she'd decided that people actually had very few choices in their lives. Most things happened to you. Most things rolled right over you and then kept on going.

"Get her the pizza, if that's what she wants," Frances told Gretel. "Let her enjoy herself."

That night, Gretel's grandmother had a terrible case of indigestion, but she didn't care. Her doctor had warned her not to have salt, sugar, fat, MSG, Tabasco, wine, spices, or anything cooked in oil. But the following day, when Gretel came home from school, Frieda was waiting for her with the menu from the Chinese take-out place up on the turnpike, a place called Ho Ho's known for its especially hot, oily food. It was years since Frieda had last tasted three-spice chicken, and nearly a decade since she'd dared to order barbecued spareribs.

"You're kidding, right?" Gretel said when her grandmother handed over the menu.

"Make sure to get a few extra packets of soy sauce," Frieda said. "They'll give you plenty if you ask."

"This is some kind of suicide thing. That's what it is!" Gretel saw the whole picture clearly now: food used as a weapon. Grease and spice aimed directly at the heart and arteries. "Well, I'm not going to participate, Grandma, so don't ask me."

"Fine." Frieda had faced down a lot tougher customers than her little pip-squeak granddaughter. Who had called her son-in-law a liar right to his face when he said he couldn't afford to pay child support? Who had taken a cab out to his fancy new house when the checks were late? "If you don't want to go, fine. They deliver."

That night they all sat on the edge of Frances's bed, with plates of Chinese food on their knees. There was an old movie on, *Now, Voyager,* and Gretel and her mother were both crying so hard they could hardly chew. Gretel's brother, Jason, who continued to be less verbal and more handsome—as if the two traits were genetically linked—rolled his eyes as he finished up the spareribs.

Grandma Frieda nudged Jason. "They think crying's going to get them someplace. It's not going to get you anyplace," she told her daughter and granddaughter.

"Oh, Mom." Frances put down her dinner plate. She

couldn't take her eyes off Bette Davis. She couldn't stop thinking about the man who'd abandoned her. "Leave us alone."

"Never," Grandma Frieda said.

As it turned out, the Chinese food seemed to have no ill effects on Frieda's digestive system. The following day she took off to Atlantic City with her canasta-playing cronies to see if they could make a killing at the Tri-State Championships. They went once a year, and although they hadn't made a killing yet, they still had hope.

When the time came, Gretel went out to the front stoop to wait for the taxi that would take her grandmother to the bus station.

"Don't you have a suitcase?" she asked when Frieda came out of the house with only a purse.

"Who needs the extra baggage?" The taxi was approaching and Frieda signaled wildly to the driver, even though there were no other people on the street. "Listen, honey," she said to Gretel just before she got into the cab. "I'm not really leaving you." Facts were facts—Gretel was her favorite, and there were tears in Frieda's eyes.

"You think crying's going to get you someplace?" Gretel teased.

She hugged her grandmother and stood out on the curb so she could wave goodbye. She waved and she waved until she couldn't see the taxi anymore; then she sat down on the edge of the curb and cried.

Frieda died that night at the Copper Penny Motel, the place where she and her girlfriends always stayed in Atlantic City, since the rooms were clean and breakfast was free—a bagel, eggs any way you liked them, and what the management vowed was fresh-squeezed orange juice. On the evening when she died, all the canasta cronies had gone to a Hungarian restaurant, and Frieda's friends wondered if it was the chicken Paprikash that had done her in, although the official coroner's report suggested that Frieda had a congenital heart defect—it had simply taken eighty-odd years to affect her.

Now when Gretel came home from school in the afternoons, she locked herself in her room. There were times when nothing seemed to matter, and this appeared to be one of them. A girl had to care if she was to comb her hair, eat a decent meal, wash her face with Ivory soap. Gretel no longer gave a damn about any of it. What was life anyway? Only a continuous vale of sadness and tears. Such were the thoughts she was entertaining, and perhaps this is why Gretel began to fade. She grew paler and paler until you couldn't quite distinguish her form when she leaned against a white wall. Frances became truly alarmed. At last she telephoned her ex and demanded he do something.

"What can I do?" Sam said, always the same sad song. "Gretel's been incorrigible from day one."

"Listen, mister, you can do plenty. Offer to send her on a trip. Buy her a new wardrobe. Invite her to your house for dinner."

After she slammed down the phone, Frances felt elated. She didn't think about her ex once that night; she didn't shed a tear. Frankly, it pleased her that she had sounded so much like Frieda all the while she'd been shouting at that self-centered loser. Naturally, of all Frances's suggestions, Sam chose the dinner invitation. What did it cost him? Two extra steaks thrown on the broiler? Another head of lettuce added to the salad? On the designated evening, Jason drove Frances's car, a rusty Ford with the rear end smashed in. As they neared the North Shore, the houses seemed bigger with every block. They kept the windows rolled down; all the same they couldn't seem to get enough air.

"We'll eat and we'll split," Jason said. "In and out."

"Yeah, yeah," Gretel said. Now she knew what people meant when they said they were in the grip of depression. She was in the grip, all right, and it was holding her tight. "Whatever."

"A total of forty-five minutes." Every time he spoke, the skin beneath Jason's left eye twitched. It was subtle, but if you looked closely you could see his discomfort, clear as day. "Fifty minutes tops. We're polite, we let the old man drop some cash on us, and we're gone."

They left their mother's car parked beneath a white birch tree, and walked across the lawn. It was November, that quiet, gray time of the year when you feel like holding someone's hand. Gretel had her own hands clasped together, like a corpse. Jason kept his hands in his pockets. The house really was huge, and maybe that was why it took so long for anyone to come to the front door.

"Fuck it, it's freezing out here," Jason said.

"Ashes to ashes," Gretel said.

"Will you cut it out?" Jason put his hand on the doorbell and left it there. "Everybody dies, Gret. Fact of life."

"Is that supposed to cheer me up?" Gretel asked. "Because somehow it just doesn't."

It was Thea who answered the door. She always seemed vaguely distraught to come face-to-face with Gretel and Jason, as if their very existence made the world a shakier place.

"Right on time," Thea said.

Actually, they were twenty minutes late, but who was counting? So what if the steaks were a little dry and the salad wilted? Gretel and Jason followed their father's new wife through the front hall, toward the dining room. There were good carpets on every floor and the furniture was highly polished.

"She's getting fat," Gretel whispered to her brother when they stopped beside the closet to take off their coats. "Look at her."

Jason glanced over his shoulder, then shrugged. "She seems the same to me."

Females over the age of nineteen never really entered his field of vision, but when their father came to join them in the dining room, even Jason noticed that he'd gained weight. Maybe his new bulk was what made Sam too uncomfortable to hug his children or welcome them to his house, or maybe it was just his true nature to merely nod coldly, suggesting they all sit down to dinner.

"What a tubster," Jason whispered to Gretel. "So much for the fitness king."

These days, Gretel wasn't eating much; she was too depressed for the comfort of food. She refused the steak—but when she took a bite of baked potato she was truly surprised. "There's tons of butter on this," she declared.

Thea laughed. "Completely wrong. Potatoes have a natural sweetness, if you cook them right. I don't even add margarine."

Gretel couldn't help but smile. No wonder they were getting fat. She took a forkful of green beans and chewed carefully. Drenched in butter.

"I think I'll get myself a glass of water," Gretel said, excusing herself from the table in spite of the desperate look Jason gave her. He'd just have to rise to the wretched task of chatting up Thea and their father alone. Gretel knew it was all Jason could do to complete a whole sentence in their father's presence, and she pitied him, but frankly, she had better things to do. She went directly to the kitchen, where a row of arched windows overlooked the wide lawn and the tiered herb garden. Gretel peeked into the refrigerator and found nothing particularly suspicious—diet soda, turkey roll, vegetables, fruit. A fat-free cheesecake sat on the counter, still in its box, and beside the cake was a pitcher which held a sauce of sugar-free cherries. And yet, when Gretel opened the oven there was the unmistakably rich odor of butter. She dragged her finger in a puddle collecting on the oven door; when she touched it to her tongue, she knew she was right. Definitely butter.

Somebody was sabotaging the food, turning the low-cal into megacal. Gretel started to have a tingling sensation in her shoulders and arms. It was the sort of feeling you have when you believe something, yet know you can't possibly be right. She thought she saw her grandmother in the pantry. Truly, she did. If it hadn't been such a ridiculous notion, Gretel would have sworn that her grandmother was rearranging the cans and jars right then. Everything Thea had set into alphabetical order was being reorganized into food groups: The pickled items were together. The legumes were relegated to a separate section. The soups all stood in a row, from tomato to salt-free chicken-noodle.

Gretel squinted, but the image was hazy no matter how she tried to focus. Still, wasn't that her grandmother's good black dress? Weren't those the gold earrings Frieda had gotten on sale at Fortunoff?

"Grandma?" Gretel said.

Even if she could have responded, the image that appeared to be Gretel's grandmother was too busy to speak. She was unscrewing the tops of jars where Thea kept her granola, her popcorn, her caramel-flavored rice cakes. To each she added a stick of butter. Frieda's supply of butter seemed endless; all she had to do was reach into her pocket and out came stick after stick.

Gretel had never felt prouder of her grandmother. She smiled broadly, and although it seemed impossible, her grandmother smiled right back. Of course, this was difficult to gauge for certain as the image had now left the pantry and was headed for the counter where the cheesecake was waiting. When the image passed by, Gretel smelled something that reminded her of a rainy day. It was a scent so piercing and sweet it might have been an embrace. If her grandmother chose to add hot pepper flakes to the cherry sauce, well then, who was Gretel to argue? She was merely respecting the wishes of the dead when she walked back to the table, and she stopped only once, to whisper in her brother's ear.

"Take my advice," she suggested. "Skip dessert."

Fate

On our street everything turned green in its own time, first the poplars and the lilacs, then the tender shoots of the iris my mother planted beside the patio the year before, when she thought she was dying. We had made a deal with the higher powers that if she lived to see the iris in the spring, she'd go on living, she'd be free and clear, and we were hopeful since spring was already here. But you can't make deals for everything; sooner or later you have to pay, and that was what seemed to be happening to my best friend Jill.

In Franconia, there wasn't a female between the ages of twelve and eighteen who wouldn't have been willing to change places with Jill for an hour or a day. We were all jealous of her, and for good reason. She had long blond hair and a sugar-sweet voice that made the boys crazy; she could eat five cupcakes without gaining an ounce. People were drawn to her, but they resented her too. They thought she had been granted more than her rightful share. Because Jill was my best friend, I spent a lot of time defending her. There were many who wanted to believe she was only beautiful on the outside, and that inside she was horrible and withered. They wanted to hear that in her heart of hearts she was as mean as a snake, she was a competitive bitch, a nightmare, a diva. But in fact, Jill was much too kind and generous. Whatever she had was yours, no questions asked. She cried at the drop of a hat, and embraced you just as quickly. She'd do almost anything if she saw a tear in your eye, and if you pleaded for mercy you'd win her over instantly, which was what had happened with Eddie LoPacca.

Jill didn't dare tell me she was pregnant until early spring; she was so thin I never would have guessed anything was amiss, except that she seemed teary, which she chalked up to allergies, or maybe a cold—her excuses varied each day. But one afternoon, when we were over at her house, the truth was revealed after we'd gone into the kitchen for a snack. It was a perfect kitchen; Jill's mother was so fanatical about cleaning we could practically eat off the floor. I coveted that kitchen so badly I could feel my skin turning green whenever I walked into the room. The spices were set out in alphabetical order. I could see my own reflection in the sink. I wanted to live there even more than I wanted to look like Jill.

I couldn't think of my own kitchen without shivering. All hell had broken loose there, and it showed. After my father left, and my mother was diagnosed with cancer, our cousin Margot had suggested that she and my mother go into business together. They now had a catering company, although neither was much of a cook. They did bar mitzvahs and engagement parties, and there were weekends when hundreds of Swedish meatballs simmered on our stove. Cleaning up after themselves was a low priority for Margot and my mother. They had both recovered from cancer scares, failed marriages, and lost hope; in their opinion, dirt could wait. They took the money they earned from catering and bought high-heeled shoes and went to the Poconos on holiday weekends looking for husbands. They didn't care how thick the grime was on our stove. *You'll see,* they vowed, *someday you won't care either,* but that day had not yet arrived.

Delighted to be in Jill's perfect kitchen, I went to the snack drawer, where her mom always had brownies and cookies. It was pure chance that I happened to look up to see Jill standing in front of the open refrigerator. They must have had liver the night before at supper, because that was what she was reaching for. I felt a chill on the back of my legs. Jill usually wept to think of lambs and calves led to slaughter. She had to close her eyes whenever I ordered a hamburger, rare.

"You're eating that?" I asked.

"This?" Jill looked at the liver as though she'd been hypnotized and was just now surfacing to consciousness. She'd already taken a bite though, and was forced to chew and then swallow.

"Are you all right?"

"I guess I felt faint," Jill admitted. "I thought it would help to have some protein." She sat down at the table and I brought her a knife and fork. She ate the liver and tears rolled down her face. Slaughtered calves no longer mattered to her. That's when I knew.

"No," I said. "Tell me you're not."

"I am." Jill nodded her beautiful head and kept on crying.

This was bad news indeed. Her boyfriend, Eddie LoPacca, was the boy that everyone wanted, but not for keeps. He was gorgeous and stupid, and for two years straight I'd written all his term papers, so I certainly knew the state of his mind. Blank as the pages in his notebook. Even my brother, Jason—who was actively screwing up his own life with Eddie's sister, Terry, as his constant companion—would come home from the LoPaccas' house shaking his head.

"That Eddie," he'd say. "No one's yet informed him that the earth is round. He thinks Abraham Lincoln is a brand of toothpaste. If you watch him closely you can actually see steam coming out of his ears when he tries to concentrate."

We had some good laughs at Eddie's expense, but when I really thought it over, I always felt sobered by the hand of fate. My brother was the one who was supposed to be such a genius, but he and Eddie were now both employed in the same deli department, so who was the real idiot? Fate could twist you around and around, if you weren't careful. Just when you thought you knew where you were headed, you'd wind up in the opposite direction or flattened against a wall.

All the same, Jill was my best friend and I wanted to help. At that point I still believed that I knew as much as most people, and more than many. That afternoon, I went home and called my cousin Margot out to the patio, where we could speak privately. She and my mother had been experimenting with napoleons and éclairs and there was bitter-sweet chocolate streaked along Margot's arms. They had a wedding on Sunday that was driving them crazy.

"I told your mother we shouldn't do weddings." Margot was supposed to have stopped smoking, but occasionally she had a Salem, during times of stress. She was having one now. "A bar mitzvah, a party, they're something else completely. At weddings people are so on edge. They can see their lives passing before their eyes. They're shutting the gate, they're locking it twice, and they turn all their anxiety into complaining about the catering. 'You call this coffee? You call this cake?' That's what we'll be hearing. Believe me."

My mother was busy rolling out dough, so Margot let me take a puff of her Salem. I thought about the way my father had dragged out leaving us. For two years my parents fought day and night, like pit bulls trapped in an L-shaped living room, but Margot's husband had vacated in a totally different style. He took off in the middle of the night; he didn't even bother to pack a suitcase, he just got into their Ford Mustang and headed south. Margot eventually got the Mustang back, but ever since her marriage had broken up, her mouth had a funny look to it, as though someone had grabbed her by the lips and yanked, hard.

When I asked her what she would do if she wanted to get rid of a baby, Margot's mouth looked even more pinched than usual. She pointed her Salem at me. "You?"

"A friend," I said.

"Sure, sure." Margot shook her head sadly. "That's what they all say."

There were actually tears in her eyes. To be honest, I felt flattered. I could hardly get a boy to look at me. All right, they'd look, they'd even take me out, but no one asked me for a second date. I was too nasty, a real wise guy, and all the boys could tell what was beneath my rotten disposition. Down deep, I wanted a commitment with a capital *C*. To get anywhere with me, a boy would have to sign his undying loyalty with his own blood.

"I swear," I told Margot. "It's for a friend."

Later, while my mother was boxing up the pastries, Margot gave me an address in New Jersey. She scribbled down all the information, dotting her *i*'s with little hearts.

"I hope your friend has money. It costs three hundred bucks." Margot was getting her coat on, a soft camel's hair I greatly admired. She didn't believe in girls getting rid of babies, but then again, she didn't believe in women working either and here she was with no husband and her own business. "I could lend you the cash," she said.

"It's not for me," I insisted.

Margot took my face in her hands and looked into my eyes. "Swear to me on your father's grave you're not pregnant."

My father was living in a huge Tudor house in Great Neck, but I swore on his grave anyway and Margot must have believed me because she kissed me on both cheeks.

"Good girl," she said, which, to my ears, sounded something like a curse.

That evening, my brother came home from the Food Star with salami and a bucket of coleslaw. He did this most nights; my mother, after all, was too busy catering to fix dinner, and that evening she actually had a date. Her first. I sat on her bed, ate a sandwich, and helped pick outfits—her black dress was too reminiscent of mourning; the red skirt was too extreme. Finally, we settled on a pale blue suit and a cream-colored blouse.

"I must be crazy," my mother said as she viewed herself in the full-length mirror. Margot had arranged this blind date, so my mother probably had reason to worry, especially since the guy was the ex-husband of Margot's next-door neighbor. But desperate times called for desperate measures, and the man in question walked, talked, and breathed—what more could you ask for?

"Well, you look great," I told my mother, which was really the truth. Her hair was short and bouncy, and you'd never guess what she'd been through, how all summer she'd been so weak she could hardly get out of bed. When she left, I went into the kitchen to fix another sandwich, but Jason had eaten all the salami, so I stole two of the éclairs from the box in the fridge. Unfortunately, the cream inside tasted like glue.

"What would you do if Terry got pregnant?" I asked my brother when he came into the room. I thought I was making idle conversation until I could go over and give Jill the address in New Jersey, but Jason went nuts. He accused me of spreading rumors, of listening to gossip and butting into his business.

"It was a hypothetical question," I informed Jason when he had stopped shouting and sat down across from me. "Or so I thought."

Jason was wearing a white shirt and had forgotten to remove his Food Star name tag. He'd won every science award in the county, but here he was, sitting across from me in our kitchen, which still smelled like chocolate and flour.

"Terry is driving me crazy," my brother said. "All she wants is a commitment."

I understood. The capital *C*. The signature in blood. As if it meant anything. As if it ever could. As if fate couldn't rattle and roll you however and whenever it pleased.

Before I went over to Jill's, I cleaned our kitchen. I used steel wool on the stove and mopped the floor twice. I scoured the sink, but it was pretty scratched up from those huge vats my mother and Margot had been using for Swedish meatballs.

"What have you been doing?" Jill asked me when I got to her house. "You have dishpan hands."

She'd been waiting for me out on the front porch, and once I arrived we headed to the schoolyard, two blocks away, where we always went to talk.

"When I live alone I'll only use paper plates," I said.

"I want white china," Jill told me. "Pure white with a gold band along the edge."

Spring was coming more slowly than usual that year; the forsythia came to bud, but waited to bloom. I thought of my mother, out on her date. I knew why she insisted on catering weddings. My mother still believed in true love. At this very instant, she was sitting across from a stranger in a rear booth of the steak house on the turnpike, wondering if it was happening to her right then and there. Was she falling for him as they ordered their salads? Were there stars in her eyes?

"I bet I never get married," I said as we opened the gate to our old playground.

"Of course you will." Jill had a dreamy look on her face. It was twilight and all the birds were singing.

"No," I said. My hair was cut so short then that when a breeze came up behind us, the back of my neck became shivery. "I don't think I ever will."

"There's someone for everyone," Jill insisted.

She was a romantic too. There was nothing you could do once a romantic was convinced fate was working in some mysterious way. I knew that for a fact. When I gave her the address my cousin Margot had scrawled, Jill smiled and placed it in her pocket, but I could tell she wasn't interested. By then, she was already planning her wedding, the sort of affair that was much too elaborate for my mother and Margot to cater. There'd be a cocktail hour, with hot and cold hors d'oeuvres, and a sit-down roast beef dinner and a huge dessert table with elaborate pastries my mother and Margot had no hope of ever perfecting.

I couldn't help but think about the way we'd come to this same exact place when we were little. Jill was afraid of heights, so she always wrapped her arms tightly around the swings' iron chains, as if that would do any good. Even back then you could tell she was going to be beautiful. We used to stay out much too late, and catch it from our mothers. We'd still be out long after the ice cream truck had gone by, ringing its bell; long after the sky was inky and black. We used to tell each other everything, but that was over now. The best we could do was stay a little while longer. We swung back and forth without much effort, without a word, until Jill tilted her head back and pointed out what should have been obvious to me if I'd bothered to look. Above us, in the dark night, we could already see stars.

Bake at 350°

The summer before my senior year in high school I made the mistake of working for my mother and my cousin Margot's catering business, the address of which happened to be our kitchen. It was the most scorching summer ever recorded in New York State. Elderly people were being warned not to venture outside; there wasn't a single air conditioner or fan to be bought at Sears or any of the hardware stores up on the turnpike, not at any price. No rain had fallen for ten weeks, and the air had turned crackly with dry heat. Whenever you snapped your fingers little white sparks skidded off your skin. When birds took flight they singed their feathers and in no time fell to the ground.

But the heat couldn't stop weddings and bar mitzvahs and christenings, not in our town, and Margot and my mother were doing so well they decided to give their business a name and have cards printed up. They called their company Two Widows, a big joke since both their husbands were not only alive and well but married to younger women. Margot, especially, cooked with such passion you'd have thought it was the heart of her ex she was sautéing instead of mushrooms for a strudel. Margot was ten years younger than my mother and fifteen years older than me, and she'd been through a lot. She'd married in her senior year of high school—like a dope, she always said. But the truth was, when she spoke of Tony, her ex, her face was so vulnerable I couldn't stand to look.

"Hey, I'll get over it," she insisted, but neither my mother nor I were convinced. Margot still telephoned Tony for reasons even she couldn't explain. If he answered she'd simply hang up, then lock herself in the bathroom and cry. But if it was the new wife, she'd become oddly invigorated; she'd let go of a string of curses you wouldn't believe.

"Where'd you learn that stuff?" I asked her. Some of the curses weren't even in English, but you could easily get their drift. That new wife's skin was probably crawling whenever the phone rang; she probably checked the windows and double-locked the doors after Margot called.

"That's for me to know and for you to never find out,"

Margot said. "Just be careful when you pick a husband. Remember what happened to me and your mother."

We were making noodle kugel that week for the Grossmans' engagement party and the oven was always turned on high. It was so hot that I'd lost six pounds without even trying. If I kept drinking quarts of water and sweating, I'd reach my ideal weight by September. Maybe then, my life would start. Something would finally happen to me. I'd fall in love. I'd move a thousand miles away. I'd wake every day and know there was a reason to get out of bed.

Lately, I'd been thinking a lot about love and marriage. My friend Jill had gotten married in the spring, and her baby was due in August. Jill hadn't bothered to finish eleventh grade and now she and Eddie LoPacca were living in the basement of her parents' house. Was this love? That's what I wanted to know. Was this destiny? Whenever I went to visit, Eddie was out with his friends and Jill was reading magazines with a glazed look in her eyes. Sometimes, she didn't even bother to glance up when I spoke. Whatever world she had entered, it was definitely a scary place.

The last few times I'd gone over, I'd sat upstairs in the kitchen with Jill's mother, who was often folding laundry and crying. Jill's mother was fanatically neat, and her new son-in-law redefined the concept of slobbery. You could smell his dirty socks from two rooms away; it didn't matter how great-looking he was, all Jill's mother could see were the rims of permanent grease under his fingernails and the chewed-up toothpicks he left on her newly sponged countertops.

"Is this what she wanted?" Jill's mother asked the last time I sat with her in the kitchen.

In all honesty, the answer was yes. Jill had wanted a baby forever, though I'd never been certain why, and I guess Eddie was part of that bargain. Or maybe she loved him, who was I to say? I, who knew nothing, was the last to sit in judgment of another's happiness and joy, even if it did include Eddie and a lot of morning sickness. I was only beginning to figure things out, and I obviously needed a great deal of help.

"How do you know the difference between a good kisser and a bad kisser?" I asked my cousin Margot, always my personal expert on love. We had pulled all the noodle kugels out of the oven. They were supposed to be cooling on the linoleum countertop, but it was so hot in the kitchen they still appeared to be baking; each pan bubbled and sizzled like a swarm of bees.

"Oh, my God, that's so easy." Margot took off her apron and pursed her mouth, considering how to best explain. "If he closes his eyes, he's good. And the bigger his tongue, the better. Sizewise, it will let you know how big his equipment is." Margot lit a Salem and fanned the smoke into the heavy, brutal air. "You know what I'm talking about, right?"

"Of course I do," I said haughtily, although I wasn't completely clear.

"Some people don't believe in the tongue measurement system. They think the size of a man's doo-dah relates to the size of his heart, but you can't prove that by me. It certainly wasn't true in Tony's case. He didn't even have a heart."

I could tell by the wistful look on Margot's face that she wouldn't notice if I took one of her Salems, so I did. The kitchen smelled of sugar and raisins and smoke. I wanted to know everything. I wanted to be prepared for what I was to face, hopefully, in September, when boys who never took notice of me before fell madly in love after just one look.

"Well, what if you're already in love with someone and then you find out they're a terrible kisser?"

"You'll dump him," Margot assured me. "And if you're too shy to do it, I'll call him and dump him for you."

"Don't talk to Margot about love," my mother said when she came into the room.

But of course, my mother was a romantic, in spite of all she'd been through. She smiled when she saw couples kissing out by the creek; her skin flushed whenever she glimpsed a newborn baby in its carriage.

That day, in the kitchen, my mother grabbed the Salem from my hand and put it out in the sink. "Love is real," she told me. "Do you understand what I'm saying? It's like a plate or a cup or a night table. That's how real it is."

"Yeah, right." Margot laughed out loud. "It's as real as the lasagna we have to fix for the Dorrios' wedding. His second," she whispered to me. "And no one knows what happened to wife number one."

"She's a travel agent in Lynbrook," my mother told Margot. "For your information."

"Well, goody for her." Margot had never wanted to do weddings in the first place. It was my mother who had always insisted. "I'll bet the way her feet hurt at the end of a day is a whole lot realer to her than love ever was."

Margot could talk as tough as she wanted, but I knew she was looking for love. Just the week before, we'd done a fiftieth-anniversary party at the Franconia Steak House, providing the petits fours and the sheet cakes, and Margot had chatted up all the good-looking waiters. Every time we went to Jones Beach, she'd check her lipstick in the rearview mirror before getting out of the car, just in case. No matter how she protested, she hadn't even begun to give up on men.

"So is Eddie a really good kisser?" I asked Jill later that day, when the purple dusk was sifting between the poplar trees and the temperature was still past ninety.

"Compared to what?" Jill said.

We were out in her parents' backyard, sitting in a wading pool we had dragged out of the garage and filled with cold water from the hose. With Jill's belly so big, we filled up the whole pool, and had to take turns stretching out our legs.

"Okay, tell me this." I was smoking a Salem I'd stolen from Margot, and I held the cigarette between my thumb and forefinger, the way Margot always did when she wanted to make a point. "What do you think about when he kisses you?"

"Are you doing a survey?" Jill had gained nearly fifty pounds, but the weird thing was, she was just as beautiful as ever, so pale in the dusky light that she almost glowed.

"All right. The truth? When he kisses me my mind goes completely blank."

We both laughed then, hard enough so that streams of water began to slosh over the sides of the pool.

"Maybe that's why I married him. Maybe I didn't want to think."

We mulled that over as fireflies appeared on the lawn.

"I wish I was ten years old," Jill said.

"Me too," I agreed. But that was a lie. I couldn't wait till September when I'd be a senior and my entire world would change.

Jill wrinkled her beautiful nose. "The whole neighborhood smells like tomato sauce."

"We're doing lasagna. There's a wedding at the Knights of Columbus Hall tonight."

We heard Eddie pull into the driveway. He had a Camaro that drove Jill's mother crazy, and to be honest it did sound more like a jet than a Chevrolet. Eddie worked down at the Food Star with my brother and I couldn't bring myself to tell Jill that employees of the deli department spent their lunch hour smoking pot in the parking lot. She thought Eddie was working so hard, slicing bologna or whatever it was they did in the deli, and who was I to destroy that dream? I was fairly certain that given time, she'd be disappointed enough in Eddie without my reports.

"Two beautiful girls, that's what I need," Eddie said.

He was a liar, but he was a good one. He'd brought home a six-pack of beer, which he dumped into the wading pool; then he sat down on the grass and eased off his boots. I could understand Jill's mother's complaint about the aroma of his socks, which he quickly pulled off so he could stick his feet in the pool.

"Your brother's quite the pisser," Eddie said to me as he got himself a beer.

My brother lately seemed to concentrate all his attention on alcohol and illegal drugs.

"He managed to get an entire delivery of beer into the trunk of his car and he was brought up to be a good sharer."

It was my mother's car actually, an ancient monster which was always in need of resuscitation.

"Thank you, Jason." Eddie raised his beer can to the sky.

"Gretel was just asking me about the way you kissed," Jill said.

She was that way sometimes, embarrassing you to death.

"Jill!" I was pretty much mortified, but I had cultivated a snooty look to ease myself out of embarrassing moments such as this.

Eddie liked this information; he thought quite highly of himself.

"Oh, yeah?" he said.

I realized that he was sitting too close to me, and now he leaned closer still.

"Want to find out?" he said.

Jill let out a snort.

"I mean it," Eddie said, although whether he was addressing me or Jill I couldn't tell. Before I could figure it out, Eddie had started to kiss me. It was getting even darker by then, and from the corner of my eye I could see

Jill's hair, which looked silvery against the sky. Eddie kissed me and went on kissing me until I couldn't breathe, and then he backed away and laughed. I must have had a stupid expression on my face, because Eddie took one look and said, "I guess I'm even better than I thought I was."

Jill was patting my leg. "Gretel?" Her voice was concerned, but I was the one who wasn't listening now. I got out of that pool fast, threw my T-shirt and shorts on over my wet bathing suit, and went to the gate. I didn't bother to retrieve my shoes, although the concrete was still burning-hot, even now, in the dark. I was late for the Dorrios' wedding, and my mother and Margot had already loaded up Margot's car and driven to the Knights of Columbus Hall. As I ran there, I thought that human beings really didn't have a chance. I kept feeling Eddie's kiss, as if it were happening over and over as I ran across lawns and headed for the turnpike. I understood why Jill looked so dumbstruck and glazed; how could she not be puzzled that a kiss had taken her so far? No wonder people did such stupid things for love. No wonder they wound up ruining their lives, or at least setting them on a strange and unknown course.

I was completely out of breath when I got to the Knights of Columbus Hall. The parking lot was full and the moon was climbing past the asphalt-shingled roof. The heat seemed to be rising, and in the back room, where my mother and Margot had set up a makeshift kitchen, the temperature must have been well over a hundred.

"Finally," my mother said when she saw me, shoeless, in damp clothes. "I was worried."

"I forgot the time." I grabbed an apron. Margot had had the Two Widows logo printed on the blue cloth.

"It's wild out there," Margot said, coming in from the function room with an empty tray. She'd been serving hors d'oeuvres, but she looked as though she'd been doing battle. "They're drinking whiskey sours like they were water."

I could tell from Margot's breath that she'd had one herself. I helped her load up another tray of hors d'oeuvres—little hot dogs wrapped in phylo dough and mini knishes—while my mother got the main course ready. If I wasn't mistaken, Margot seemed a little flushed, and when I followed her into the wedding party I saw the reason why. There was a man who was searching the room, and when he saw Margot he waved.

"Hey, baby," he called.

Margot turned to me and for an instant I saw the hope in her eyes. I saw that she'd be willing to try again; she'd do anything for love, the real sort, the sort that would last.

"Wish me luck," she whispered.

I was standing beside the bar, which specialized in whiskey sours and rum punch, and I could see her all the way across the room. I couldn't help but wonder what this man's history was; if he'd been married, or if he was married still. For all we knew, he could be Dorrio himself, today's bridegroom. Not that it mattered. There he was, on the other side of the room. There she was, headed straight for him. And there I stood, barefoot, in the Knights of Columbus Hall, during the hottest summer of our lives.

True Confession

In the darkest hour of winter, when the starlings had all flown away, Gretel Samuelson fell in love. It happened the way things are never supposed to happen in real life, like a sledgehammer, like a bolt from the blue. One minute she was a seventeen-year-old senior in high school waiting for a Sicilian pizza to go; the next she was someone whose whole world had exploded, leaving her adrift in the Milky Way, so far from earth she was walking on stars.

She'd been daydreaming, staring through the plate-glass window, her arms on the countertop, not even noticing that someone had arrived to pick up his order. When she thought about it later though, she'd felt him there, a heat wave beside her. She couldn't have kept herself from falling in love with him; she never had a chance. Before she realized he was next to her, he had placed his hand over hers on the countertop, then looped his fingers through hers. Gretel looked up at him, so startled she might as well have been shot.

"I just wanted to wake you up," he said.

Which is exactly what he did. One look at him and her heart was racing. One look, and whatever her life had been before was all over.

His name was Sonny Garnet and she had heard about him in the way people hear about a skirmish in a far-off country, someplace war-torn and dangerous. He'd been picked up for questioning by the police half a dozen times, he'd been tried and let go, stolen cars had been involved, or was it drugs, or was it a cop who had been paid off? None of it was true, he told Gretel now. It was idle gossip, jealous speculation. He was only twenty-two, but he seemed unbelievably adult. He had a wallet filled with cash and a brand-new Camaro; he had a way of taking your hand which made it clear he'd have to be the one to let go.

He paid for the meatball sub he had ordered, but Gretel knew he was waiting for her in the vestibule, and she was trembling when she picked up her pizza; she was holding the box too tightly, surely the cheese would slide off the top, but she didn't care. She'd had the funniest feeling when she looked at him the first time, and it happened again when he opened the door for her. She was somehow blinded, as if Sonny Garnet were made not out of plodding flesh and blood like other men, but of clear true light. Was he exceptional-looking? She never could tell. He had dark hair and pale blue eyes with features so wary and sharp they gave the impression that he never needed sleep. He was tall, and had to bend to be on eye level with most people, but he did this so gracefully any girl he spoke to had the sense that she was the only person in the world, and that talking to her was more important than breathing, than seeing, than life itself.

"I couldn't leave you here," Sonny Garnet said to Gretel as she hugged the pizza box tighter, so close it nearly burned her skin.

"Why not?" Gretel was a practical girl, and liked to know the score. She was careful too, or so she thought.

"Because I knew I'd regret it," Sonny said.

Gretel looked at him and blinked. She wondered if she had grown extremely stupid. Why was it that she trusted what he was saying? How was it possible for her to believe every word?

Sonny was so smooth he could have a person walking toward his parked car before she knew where she was headed. He could open the door and help her inside before she realized she'd made a decision. As soon as he got behind the wheel, Gretel should have known what she was letting herself in for, but maybe a broken heart seemed a simple price to pay, the way all costs that must be settled in the future appear, until they suddenly come due.

When he let her off in her driveway, Gretel's cousin Margot was just arriving. Margot stood on the front stoop and watched Gretel slowly unfold herself from the Camaro, carrying the pizza carelessly, as though it were the last thing on her mind.

"There goes trouble," Margot said as Sonny Garnet drove away.

Gretel could almost believe that the ice coating the sidewalk was melting beneath her feet. She would have spoken, but words were impossible; the only thing that would form in her mouth was a sigh.

"Well, baby, you have got yourself a problem," Margot said to Franny when she came into the kitchen. Margot plopped down the dozen cookbooks she'd brought over, then took off her gloves and scarf and draped them over a kitchen chair. "Get ready for the shit to hit."

In Frances's opinion Margot always overreacted, but when she went into the living room and saw the pizza deposited on an easy chair and her daughter staring into the mirror above the couch as though she'd been hypnotized, Frances thought there might, indeed, be cause for concern. She touched Gretel's forehead for fever and was delighted to find she was burning-hot. That, at least, was a predicament that could be solved.

"Take two aspirin and go to bed," Frances said.

"Okay." Gretel was as docile as a lamb, and already too far gone to reach.

"She has a fever," Frances told Margot when she went back to the kitchen. "FYI."

The two cousins got together every Thursday night to trash their ex-husbands and look for new recipes for their catering business. Margot had opened *The Hallelujah Hawaiian Cookbook* to pineapple-chicken bits, but now she closed the book.

"A fever? Wake up, Franny. She's in love."

"Concentrate on your Hawaiian chicken." Frances had had enough awful things happen to her recently; another serious complication would be overkill from above. "You'll get more accomplished if you stick to business."

But Margot was never one to ignore a problem, and the next day she was waiting on the stoop at exactly three o'clock, never mind that the temperature was eighteen degrees Fahrenheit and she had to wear earmuffs and two pairs of gloves. Although it was freezing, cold enough to turn the tip of a person's nose blue, Margot was out there long enough to have smoked two Salems by the time Gretel finally arrived home from school in Sonny's car.

Margot couldn't see a thing, since the windows of the Camaro were all fogged up, but as soon as Gretel opened the car door and stumbled out, Margot could tell it would soon be too late for intervention. The look on Gretel's face was so dreamy and warm it took the chill right out of the air. She looped her arm through Margot's and together they watched Sonny Garnet's Camaro speed away. The car was a deep red color, like rubies or blood, and if you narrowed your eyes it seemed as though a bright red thread were sewing up the asphalt and the ice.

"Thirty-five minutes late getting home," Margot said.

"Sue me," Gretel told her.

"Haven't you seen enough bad luck?" Margot sighed. "Didn't you learn anything from your mother and me?"

Gretel kissed Margot on the cheek, then headed for the front door. "Get off my case. This is my life."

Margot's and Frances's divorces weren't even in the same universe as what was happening to Gretel. All those men who had dumped Margot, or had disappointed her—the most recent one having turned out to be a lot more married than he had first implied—were not the same species as Sonny Garnet. Sonny could blow all of them away; he could turn them to dust with a snap of his fingers, then pick up the pieces and put them back together again.

Gretel only had to think of him, and she was completely gone. No matter what she was doing or where she was, in her mind she was walking to his car, parked by the curb in front of the high school. She was standing in the living room of the apartment he shared with his older brother, Desmond, who was away on business until spring. Every time she closed her eyes, she felt the way she had the first time he'd kissed her. She hadn't had all that much experience with romance, and none of it prepared her for Sonny Garnet. None of it led her to expect the ledge she would fall off when he leaned close to her.

He had whispered to her before he kissed her, he had asked if it was all right, not that Gretel could have spoken. But he must have gotten his answer, because he kissed her then, so deeply she thought she would never surface from the place she had gone to, and maybe she still hadn't. Maybe she was still there, wrapped up in bliss. While she walked into the kitchen, while she ignored Margot nattering at her, while she threw her books on the counter, then poured a glass of juice and drank it all up, she was kissing him still.

"I told you she was in love," Margot announced to Frances, who was at the kitchen table, struggling to figure out her finances and pay the monthly bills.

"Don't ruin your appetite," Frances told Gretel, who'd sat down across from her to fix a peanut butter sandwich.

"Okay," Gretel said in a dreamy tone.

Frances looked up right away. Gretel was never so pliant.

"See what I mean?" Margot said. "Is this our Gretel?"

They studied her carefully as she chewed her sandwich. She looked the same; the high cheekbones, the wide mouth that was often twisted into a sneer. But something had definitely shifted; even though they loved Gretel dearly, they had always admitted she had a nasty disposition, and now the edge was gone.

"I see exactly what you mean." Frances felt little waves of fear up and down her skin. She thought of Gretel's best friend Jill Harrington, pregnant, then married in eleventh grade. Frances pushed aside her unpaid bills and considered carefully. "You're grounded," she declared.

"Why?" Gretel cried.

"An ounce of prevention," Margot informed her little cousin.

"For how long?"

"Permanently," Frances said. "Or until you break up with him."

"This isn't fair," Gretel said. "You don't even know him."

"Oh, yes we do," Margot called as Gretel ran from the room. "We know him better than you think."

Gretel locked herself in her room; she flung herself on her bed and wept until her brother brought her dinner. When Jason knocked, Gretel unlatched the door, then re-flung herself across her quilt, the dinner plate before her. It was a bologna sandwich, with mustard, and some gherkins.

"Thanks," Gretel said, uncertainly. In principle, she thought she should stage a hunger strike of some sort.

Jason leaned his head against the bedroom wall. For the past few years, he'd been so busy ruining his life he'd barely had time to talk to Gretel. Now Gretel was surprised to find he was interested.

"Sonny Garnet," he said thoughtfully. "I'm proud of you." Gretel's brother was still gorgeous and much too smart for his own good, but he'd become sly and far too skinny. "Now you'll have access to the best drugs in town."

"You wish," Gretel said. The bologna sandwich wasn't half bad. Falling in love had made her hungrier than usual; she wanted things she hadn't before, and she was embarrassed to think of all she now desired.

"Maybe you can score for me." Jason gave her his best smile, which was so good it usually did the trick. "Amphetamines are his specialty."

Gretel stopped eating. "Boy, do you have the wrong idea," she told her brother. "You're crazy."

Jason had always considered her to be naive; he now found her pathetic. "Wake up," he told her wearily.

"That's exactly what I'm doing," Gretel shouted as her brother left the room. "I'm waking up right now!"

That night she climbed out her window at midnight, and walked along the icy streets. Everything was dark blue and black, the road and the sky and the clouds. Gretel was so on fire she didn't notice the weather. She was in a state of pure desire, a condition few people experience, and even fewer survive. Sneaking out her window was nothing; disobeying her mother even less. As smart as she was, she would have done anything for Sonny Garnet. If that made her stupid, so be it. There she was, the stupidest girl in the world, who wouldn't stop until she got to his door.

The apartment was three flights up, and when Gretel knocked, the door, left ajar, opened. Sonny was on the telephone; his back was to Gretel and his shirt was off. He was wearing black slacks and his hair was wet from a shower, and Gretel knew this was the defining moment of her life. Would she stay or would she run? Was she the sort of person who would turn away from what she wanted most, and then, forever after, live with her regret? Frankly, she didn't know until she went to him and reached her arms around him.

After that, she went to his apartment whenever she could. She was so burning-hot little sparks fell from her fingertips and left their marks in the asphalt as she walked the same path every night. Her secret life began to take a toll. Words escaped her; odd things amused her. When woken from sleep, she often could not remember her own name. *This is what love is,* she thought when she was beside him. But there were times, in the morning, after she'd climbed back through her window to get into her own bed, when she could have sworn she saw the outline of her heart rising through her chest. Try as she might to steal a few pale hours of sleep, lulled by clean sheets and the waking song of the few winter birds that were left, she would suddenly panic. Her arms and legs would grow cold as ice. *I'm not ready for this,* that's what she'd think. *I'm not now, and I never will be.*

Sonny Garnet kept extremely odd hours. He slept through noon, and stayed up until dawn. Gretel knew this because twice she had told her mother she was staying at a friend's house, then had promptly gone to Sonny's to spend the night. It was all him when she was there. They didn't bother with dinner or small talk; there was no talk at all. Gretel let him do things she didn't even know people did, all because of the way he looked at her, the way he said, *I'm never going to let you go.*

Later, what she remembered most was that the phone was always ringing. All night long, it rang and rang. Every now and then there'd be a knock at the door, sometimes when they were in bed together and sometimes when she was fast asleep. Sonny always told her not to worry, not to bother; he'd take care of everything. And when he went out to the hallway and closed the door behind him, Gretel didn't think twice about what he was doing or where he'd been. But there was a night when Sonny wasn't home and someone came to the door. Gretel tried to ignore it, but the racket kept getting louder, and when she couldn't stand to hear it anymore, she threw on her clothes and opened the door. The man who was stationed there was already furious, and Gretel hadn't even said anything yet.

"Where is he?" the man demanded.

"I don't know." Although this was a fact, Gretel felt ridiculous and foolish. Somehow, she had entered into a situation where the truth felt as flimsy as a lie.

The man pushed the door open, hard, so that it slammed against Gretel's shoulder. He could have done anything to her then—murdered her, raped her—but all he did was look through the cabinets in the kitchen and go through all the drawers. When he didn't find what he wanted, he simply turned and walked out, but the way he'd shoved the door open had left a purple bruise on Gretel's skin. Afterwards, when she looked at the mark, she got a nagging feeling, as if Margot had somehow settled into her brain to remind her, again and again, that smart girls should always look before they leap.

At the end of February, on a gray and heartless day, Gretel realized that her period was late. She went over to the Harringtons' basement, where her friend Jill lived with her husband and six-month-old baby, Leonardo, named for his grandfather on his father's side. Leonardo was advanced for his age, and he crawled in a circle on the floor, like some large crustacean, while Gretel cried.

"You'll just have to make the best of it," Jill told her. "Look at me."

Gretel did and started crying again.

"Well, thanks a lot." Jill was all huffy and defensive. "My sweet little crab boy." She scooped up Leo and kissed him half a dozen times. "It's not such a bad fate."

That evening, Gretel went to Margot's house. She pounded on the front door, since the bell had broken ages ago.

"You almost gave me a heart attack," Margot said when she let Gretel in. She'd been watching the news on TV and eating chocolate-covered pretzels. The house was something of a mess, and had been for several years, ever since Tony had taken off.

"What if I was pregnant?" Gretel said tentatively.

"Oh, Jesus," Margot said. "What's wrong with you girls?"

Gretel threw herself into an easy chair. Her head was spinning. "It's just a *what if* situation."

"Okay, fine. You want a *what if?*" Margot got out her cigarettes and a diamond-studded lighter her ex had given her years before. "What if I killed you, how's that?"

"Go ahead, do it," Gretel said. "I'd thank you."

"Gretel, I thought you were smarter."

"I'm in love with him," Gretel said, as though that were an explanation for anything.

"Sure you are." Margot wasn't wearing any makeup, and she looked tired, but she was still young enough to remember how all of this felt. "Whatever you want to do," she told Gretel, "I'll stand by you."

Three days later, Gretel got her period, but instead of feeling relief, she had the oddest sense of loss. She closed up on herself. She stopped talking. When Sonny gave her an opal ring for her birthday, all she could do was sit down and cry.

"Not exactly the reaction I thought this would get," Sonny said.

There was nothing wrong with the ring. It was, by far, the most beautiful gift Gretel had ever received. She wore it day and night; she stared at it as she fell asleep and gazed upon it when she opened her eyes in the morning. But she could look at that opal all she wanted, and it still wouldn't erase the premonition she had that disaster was only steps away, and heartbreak even closer. She had started to hear the phone ring late at night at Sonny's place. She'd begun to feel an ache in her chest whenever she saw Sonny, the way people do when they know something is going to break apart.

It happened in March, just when there were hints the winter would end. The sky was bluer, the wind less like a hammer; ice had begun to melt, leaving cold, little streams in the gutters and streets. It was a Saturday and Frances and Margot were in the kitchen preparing for a Saint Patrick's Day party. They were fixing green potato knishes, éclairs filled with mint cream, and celery sticks stuffed with green-tinted tuna salad. It was noon, but no one ever ate lunch in this house. They grabbed bits and pieces, which is what Gretel did when she came into the kitchen, already wearing her navy-blue jacket.

"Where are you off to?" her mother asked her. "You're never here anymore."

Gretel had already taken two of the éclairs, and now Frances smacked her hand when she reached for a third.

"I'm just going out." Gretel saw the way Margot was looking at her, lips pursed, like she knew the answer to some state secret. "No place in particular," Gretel said, directly to Margot. "FYI."

But of course, that wasn't true. All the night before, she'd been dreaming of Sonny Garnet, and in her dream he had left her to talk on the phone. He always paced when he talked on the telephone; he wound the cord around his arm like a tourniquet. Not that he was the least bit nervous; no way. Even if you couldn't make out what he was saying, his voice sounded so smooth. But in her dream, he wasn't smooth at all. When he spoke, rocks came out of his mouth. White stones, so flawless it had taken Gretel a while to realize they weren't rocks at all, but perfect white teeth.

She'd woken that morning with a terrible urge to see him, and by noon she couldn't wait any longer. All the way there she had an odd, breakable feeling, as if the slightest thing could hurt her. A branch falling from above, a strong gust of wind, anything could destroy her or blow her off course. Ever since she'd fallen in love, the rest of her life had somehow slipped away from her, the reality of streets and trees, the future and the past—it had been soaked up in the present with Sonny Garnet. She'd never noticed the twisted crab apple which grew by the front door of his apartment building. She'd never heard the way the steps creaked as she ran up to the third floor, or paid the least bit of attention to how cold it was in the stairwell, colder than the blue, March air outside.

Just before she knocked on the door, Gretel thought to herself, *I could leave now,* but she didn't. She bit down hard on her lip, and prepared herself for whatever was to be, and still she was completely undone when a girl answered the door. She was a beautiful girl of nineteen or twenty, with long blond hair and too much makeup. Immediately, Gretel lost the ability to speak.

"What is it?" the girl said. At least her teeth were awful. She was wearing a tacky name necklace. Laura was her name, and she acted as though she owned the place. She had her hands on her hips. "What do you want?"

"Sonny," Gretel said, and alas, it was true. Standing in the hallway, where she now noticed the linoleum was cracked and filthy, she wanted him terribly.

"Well, Sonny's sleeping. You'll have to come back later."

"I can't," Gretel said. "I'm here now."

Laura came into the hall and closed the door behind her. "I wouldn't wake him up if I were you. He's already bent out of shape because I made him sleep in the living room so I could fix up the bedroom for Desmond."

As far as Gretel was concerned, this girl was speaking another language.

"Hello?" Laura said when faced with Gretel's silence. She waved her hand in front of Gretel's face. "Are you there?"

That was when Gretel started to cry. "You can't have him," she said, even though she had no idea how she would manage to fight a rival who was a grown woman with red nail polish and so much mascara.

"You think I'm here with Sonny! I'm waiting for Desmond." Another blank look from Gretel. "Sonny's brother?"

Now that she understood, Gretel threw her arms around Laura as though she were a long-lost sister, and as soon as she did Laura started to cry right along with her.

"You don't know what it's been like," Laura said as they both wept. Close up, Gretel could see Laura was older than she'd first thought. She might even be close to thirty. "It's been hell," Laura confided. "I've had to live with my mother in New Hyde Park."

They sneaked back into the apartment to have a cup of instant coffee together in the kitchen. That was when Gretel found out that Desmond Garnet had been in the Nassau County jail for the past eighteen months.

"I thought he was away on business," Gretel said.

"He was," Laura told her. "Amphetamines and crystal meth. That is his business."

Because he was older, Desmond had taken the fall. Next time, it would be Sonny's turn.

"I'm so nervous now that he's coming back," Laura admitted. "I want everything to be perfect when he gets here. Is my hair okay?"

"You look great," Gretel told her. Just tired. Just worn out from all that waiting she'd been doing.

"I'm glad Sonny finally settled down with someone too."

"We're not all that serious," Gretel heard herself insist. Why would she say that? Why would she sip her coffee as though it were true? She turned the opal ring around on her finger, to ensure that the stone wouldn't show. All this time she'd been breathing for him, or so she'd believed. Now, she wasn't even certain she knew Sonny Garnet. Who was he really? Who could he be?

"Wild men." Laura shook her head. "That's what they are. They'll do whatever they please. They'll never listen to us."

"Nope," Gretel said. The faucet in the kitchen sink was dripping. The heat was on too high. Traffic from the street echoed here, and she'd never even noticed. Gretel rinsed out her coffee cup. "I've got to go," she said.

"You definitely don't want to be here when I start the vacuum and wake Sonny up."

It was dark in the living room when Gretel walked through. All the shades were drawn and Sonny was asleep on the couch, his long legs stretched out, his face pale in the darkness. He'd set his boots right beside the couch, the way men who are used to making quick getaways always do. He looked beautiful in the dark, a creature from a distant planet. Gretel thought about the way he looked all the way home. She thought about it and thought about it, until the image shattered inside her mind into pure white light.

When she got to her house, her mother was out in the driveway, loading Margot's car with trays of green food.

"Hey, you," Frances called. "Don't wait up tonight. We'll be back late."

Margot had come out onto the front stoop with the tray of éclairs.

"Are you okay?" she asked when she saw Gretel's face.

"No." Gretel was still seeing that white light in her mind, but that would soon fade.

"He dumped you."

It was such a mild afternoon for this time of year. So hazy and so blue.

"Yes," Gretel said. The white light was fading already, if she narrowed her eyes.

"Stinker." Margot shook her head. She shifted the éclairs so she could put an arm around Gretel's shoulders. "You'll find someone better. I promise you will."

By then Gretel had the opal ring in her pocket. It was a truly delicate piece of jewelry; she wouldn't even know it was gone until she had lost it, and then she could search under carpets and radiators as often as she liked, she'd never find it again. No matter how hard she tried.

"Count your lucky stars that it's over sooner rather than later," Margot said.

Gretel shook her head so that the last remnants of white light flew up into the air and dissolved into what would soon be spring.

"All right," she said. "I'll do that."

The Rest of Your Life

One morning, when the air was misleading and mild with hope, I saw my mother standing beside the forsythia. The blossoms had just begun to open, and were now as much yellow as they were green. The branches tumbled into the yard, heavy with the weight of flowers and leaves, and there was my mother, all alone. She was smoking a cigarette, the first she'd had in years, since her cancer had first been diagnosed and treated. Her hair was dark and thick, and she hadn't bothered with a comb or a brush. She was crying out there, beside the forsythia, but even if she hadn't been, I would have known. Certain things need not be said, and there's nothing, not a whispered prayer, not a sacrifice, not a payment of any price, that will change what's about to happen.

We had dinner that night in the dark, not out of choice but because a storm had come up. The wind knocked down the power lines all over Franconia and left a dimmer world, a shadowy place where a working flashlight seemed worth its weight in gold. We stuck candles into wine bottles and waited for Margot to come over with a pizza.

"I got the last one before the oven went out." Margot had picked up some antipasto and two bottles of wine as well, one of which my mother now grabbed and began to open.

"Let's get drunk," my mother said.

Margot and I exchanged a look. My mother didn't drink.

"Okay," we agreed, and we set about it as the wind rattled down our chimney.

We didn't stop drinking until the candles had burned down. By then, there was nothing left anyway, and we hadn't the heart for wine anymore. At ten o'clock my brother came home from work. He took bad news the way some people do, with silence and distance and even more distrust in the world than he usually had. He was working double shifts at the Food Star; he was worried about medical bills and mortgages, matters no one should be considering at the age of twenty. All of his free time was spent getting high; he did drugs with a vengeance, pursuing his own destruction the way he had once gone after good grades. He should have been in college; he should have been having the time of his life. Instead, he was standing in our dark kitchen, wolfing down the last piece of pizza and giving us grief for allowing my mother to drink.

"That should be her biggest problem," Margot said.

At that point, my mother was curled up on the couch—for a nap, she had told us, but it was clear she was out for the night. If you looked at the way she was sleeping, with her knees crunched together and her back so twisted, you couldn't help but think that the world was a crueler place than anyone had ever dared to suggest. You might even find yourself believing that *fair* itself was a meaningless concept, one which would only deceive you, in the end.

Margot started to cry then, and once she did, I did too.

My brother groaned. "A lot of good that will do."

"Nothing will do any good," Margot said.

In the past few months, since my mother had found a new lump under her arm, things had moved much too fast. Maybe that's why Margot looked as if she'd aged a whole year in a matter of days. Time wasn't the same anymore. Doors were slamming shut before we even knew they'd been opened. Good fortune can take forever to get to you, but as it turns out, sorrow is as quick as a shot.

We all had hangovers the next morning, but by the time Margot had come over and I had dragged myself out of bed, my mother was already at the kitchen table, looking up cemeteries in the phone book.

"You're kidding, right?" Margot said.

My mother smiled the way she always did when she was convinced she was right. "If you don't want to go with me, fine. I'll drive myself."

"Are you going to drive yourself to your own funeral too?" Margot asked.

"I'll take a taxi." My mother reached for one of Margot's Salems. "Don't even think of telling me not to smoke," she informed her cousin. "I have a perfect right to do as I please. Considering it doesn't make a difference."

I poured myself a glass of orange juice and started to cry.

"Look what you did now, Franny," Margot said to my mother. "You made Gretel cry. Do you see what you're doing by starting to smoke again? You're sending your only daughter around the bend."

"Gretel's very sensitive," my mother said. "She always cries."

The truth was, I hadn't even realized that my mother was sick again until she began sleeping more. It wasn't just naps; she would be sitting there with you having tea one minute, and the next she'd have her head on the table, eyes closed. After that, she started losing weight, even though she ordered a chocolate milk shake and a double cheeseburger every time we went out for lunch. When she started coughing, I knew I should worry; it was the sort of cough you hear all night long, that reverberates through your dreams. My mother swore she would see a doctor, but she waited a few weeks, and then a month, and by that time she'd started to have backaches. Although we hadn't recognized it as such, that had been the sign that her cancer had not only reappeared but had already spread to her lungs.

"If Gretel is so sensitive, how come she didn't apply to college?" Margot asked. "She knows that's what you want for her. She's got two more months until high school graduation and then what's she going to do? Work at the Food Star like Jason? Deliver newspapers?"

"Can we talk about this another time?" I said.

"When?" Margot demanded to know. "When it's too late?"

"Let's not fight," I suggested, nodding at my mother, who was still looking through the listing of cemeteries.

"You call this a fight?" Margot shook her head. "Baby, you've never seen a fight if you think this is one."

"Pinelawn," my mother said, closing the phone book at last.

I started crying all over again.

"If you're going to do that, you can't come," my mother warned.

"Absolutely not," Margot agreed.

I blew my nose, and put on a pair of sunglasses.

"Now you're talking," my mother said to me, and I really did have to laugh, since I wasn't saying a word.

I sat like that, in silence, shielded by dark glasses, all the way out to Pinelawn. When we turned off the expressway, there were miles and miles of graves. It was mind-boggling to think that so many people had already died, but here they were, all in a row.

"My God," Margot said. She was driving, but she was paying more attention to the cemetery than to the road. "This goes on forever."

My mother insisted that Margot and I wait in the car while she went in to buy the plot. We smoked cigarettes and listened to the radio. We had made a vow not to cry, for my mother's sake, so instead we played a game Margot had taught me when I was little and she was my baby-sitter.

"I'm going to my grandmother's house and I'm bringing an ax," I said.

"I'm going to my grandmother's house and I'm bringing an ax and a vial of barbiturates," Margot fired back.

"That counts as *V.* For vial. If you want it to be *B* it will have to be a bunch of barbiturates."

"Fine," Margot said. "Give me a bunch. Give me a bazillion."

It was my turn now. "I'm going to my grandmother's house and I'm bringing an ax, a bunch of barbiturates, and a cure for cancer."

"Gretel." Margot sighed.

She thought I was impossible, but she loved me anyway, which is the best sort of love there is. When my mother came out of the office she looked giddy and flushed. She smelled like roses as she got into the car. She had a map of Pinelawn, a complicated document of twisted lanes and roads, which she waved under our noses.

"Vista Drive," she said. "Plot number two-two-five."

That's when she saw the cigarette in my hand.

"Are you crazy?" my mother cried. "Why would you do this to yourself?"

I had already opened the window, but before I could toss out the cigarette, my mother grabbed it away. She practically had electricity shooting out of her fingertips, and her hair stood on end.

"Don't you ever do that again! Ever!"

My mother turned to face the windshield. Her shoulders were shaking.

"Okay," I said. I might have been crying. "I won't smoke."

"Franny, it was my fault," Margot said. "I figured what the hell."

"Well, figure it differently." My mother's voice sounded small and tight. "Let's go. Vista Drive."

Margot started driving, but the cemetery was confusing and my mother had to keep directing her, and when that still didn't work, she had Margot stop the car and got behind the wheel herself. It had begun to rain by the time we finally found plot 225, the light, pale rain of spring which smells so good. We didn't have raincoats or umbrellas, but we got out anyway.

"I don't like it." Margot pursed her lips. There was a tremor around her mouth which seemed to make speaking more difficult than usual. "Not one damn bit."

"What's not to like?" my mother asked. "It's the same as all the others."

"For one thing, you're too close to your neighbors." By then Margot was crying. "Franny," she said.

Margot couldn't really say more; she was sobbing, her voice so strangled she didn't even sound like herself. Margot dipped her head as though looking for cigarettes in her purse, but she kept making the most awful noise, as if she had something stuck in her throat and she couldn't get it out, no matter how hard she tried.

"Think of it this way," my mother said. "This place may be crowded, but that just means it won't be as lonely."

Margot snorted. "You think they're having parties?"

The falling rain didn't seem clear, the way rain usually does. It was pale blue, as if the sky itself was coming down. My mother had asked for so little; it seemed to me she'd never gotten anything she'd wanted. She was the sort of person who cried at sad stories in the newspaper and truly believed in kindness, who put her arm around your shoulders for comfort, even though she was the one who was dying.

"It's pretty here," I said.

Margot gave me a look, as though I had betrayed her, but I didn't care.

"Really," I told my mother. "It's pretty."

There was a bird perched above us in a leafless tree, a little gray thing, a sparrow or a wren. We all looked up, hoping it would sing, but it was silent as stone. We had to laugh then, all three of us.

"Just our luck," Margot said. "A mute."

"Maybe it's resting," my mother insisted. "Maybe it sang the most beautiful song in the world right before we got here." The bird stared down at us from a wavering branch. "You never know."

By then, the rain was falling harder, but none of us paid the least bit of attention. We didn't even blink.

"Exactly." I had to agree. "You never can tell."

The Boy Who Wrestled with Angels

The first time Jason Samuelson met up with his fate was in September, when the lilies were fading and the air had begun to grow chilly at dusk. Later, those who loved him looked back on that day and realized that Jason's downward spiral had been happening for some time. They simply hadn't noticed what was right there in front of them, the way some people manage to overlook the sand shifting beneath their feet until an earthquake actually strikes and reveals just how unreliable the whole world can be.

When Jason collapsed on the loading dock of the Food Star, the last thing he saw was the blue sky above him, a vision so cloudless and vast that even he, a careless young man who had managed to constantly receive without ever giving in return, felt helpless and small. Jason had shot heroin into his veins in the meat locker of the supermarket where he worked, and he'd known something was wrong right away: The peace which usually settled over his soul when he got high did not come to him. Instead, he felt filled to the brim with something slithery; it was as if black toads and newly hatched snakes had been trapped beneath his skin, and now they all struggled to break free in a horrible clawing fashion that took his breath away and left him sprawled upon the asphalt.

That was where his girlfriend, Terry LoPacca, found him when she checked out of fruits and vegetables. By then, Jason's pulse had slowed and his skin was ashen. He had no idea that Terry was on the ground beside him, weeping and calling for help, or that an ambulance from Franconia Hospital would soon be on its way. Unlike many people who experience a blast of welcoming white light when death is near, Jason was surrounded by empty space, as though he'd been swept right into the sky. He was enveloped in something far more powerful than himself, and he flailed out against it. He could feel the burning, endless grip of eternity snapping down on his wrists and shaking his soul; there was a syrupy poison engulfing his heart and lungs, but he wouldn't give in. There on the loading dock, Jason fought and he fought well. He lashed out and kicked, he growled like a dog; he was not ready to die on the asphalt, between crates of bananas and canned dog food.

Four attendants and the ambulance driver were needed to restrain him and carry him off the loading dock, and even then they had to tie him to the stretcher for fear he'd break his neck as he twisted and turned. When Jason regained consciousness, three hours later in a metal bed in the emergency room, he was surrounded by women. All he could hear was the low murmur of their voices. For an instant he thought he'd lost the battle and because of some celestial error, the angels were beside him now.

"You idiot," Jason's sister said to him. Gretel was so relieved to see his eyes open that she nearly passed out herself; her face was chalky with concern. She had always looked up to her brother, but current circumstances had required her to look down and she didn't like what she saw. Didn't anyone else notice that the boy who had once had everything was quickly becoming a man who could be neither trusted nor satisfied? Terry LoPacca, always so grateful for a snippet of Jason's attention, was fawning over him, kissing his hands and his eyes, pledging her love. Gretel's mother and their cousin Margot were already considering a lawsuit against the hospital attendants, whose rough treatment had left their sweet boy with bruises on his arms and legs. Did they fail to see how much weight Jason had recently lost? Had they never realized that all the good silverware in the house had slowly been disappearing, sold for a meager profit, then displayed in a case at the pawnshop behind the shopping center? Devotion had kept them from recognizing who he had become, and even now they cooed as they tenderly untied Jason's ankles and wrists from their restraints. Even now they blamed everyone else for the troubles he'd seen. He was their darling after all, their one and only boy.

That night, Gretel sat out in their backyard and stared at the sky. She recognized Pegasus in the southern sky and for some reason this made her cry. Most of the girls she knew had gotten jobs or gone off to college, but not Gretel. She went with her mother to doctors' appointments and folded laundry. She was a girl with a forlorn nature who desperately wanted to believe in something, but so far the most she had managed to believe in was bad luck. This evening, she couldn't find her way past the black despair that wraps around those who love a person who cannot be saved. Jason came out of the house in a clean white shirt and baggy jeans; he sat down beside Gretel and lit a cigarette. In spite of everything he'd done to himself, he was still incredibly handsome. Women on the street often stopped to stare, unable to collect themselves for hours after he'd walked by; they dreamed about him for weeks if he bothered to give them a second look or a smile. He was Gretel's brother, the same flesh and blood, but every day he was more of a stranger. He'd always taken risks, but the level of danger had increased. He'd walk right into the center of anything perilous—any fight, any drug, any chance he could take. He'd do it just for the hell of it, even if the odds were so set against him anyone could tell he'd never win.

"Are you trying to kill yourself?" Gretel asked.

Jason blew out smoke. He also spied the square of Pegasus, but he paid the constellations no mind. When he tallied his reasons to live, all he could come up with were ways to numb himself.

"You are so stupid," Gretel told her brother. She hadn't expected him to respond, but that didn't mean she didn't know the answer.

"Really?" Jason stubbed out his cigarette in the flower bed where their mother had tried to grow tulips for years. Not a single one had managed to bloom. "What's the speed of light, missy?" Jason asked. "What's the square root of a hundred and forty-four?" After all he'd been through, his smile was still worth seeing. "Who's stupid now?"

"You're going to actually do it if you're not careful," Gretel warned. "Then I'll be furious."

"Gretel, if I wanted to die, I'd already be dead."

After they had both thought this over, Gretel took her brother's hand in hers, the hand that had so often bought heroin and methamphetamine up on the turnpike, the hand that had stolen from his own mother and reached for all the most beautiful girls in town, and she bit him, hard.

Jason let out a yelp and got to his feet. He looked at the teeth marks his sister had left as if he couldn't quite believe what had happened.

"I guess you're right," Gretel said. "You are still alive."

Later that night Jason almost corrected the situation when the car he was driving on a dark road through the woods spun out of control. He was behind the wheel of

Terry's red Trans Am—the one she'd been given as a graduation present—intent on forcing the speedometer to its highest level, when he noticed that the stars had shifted in the sky. The reason for this, he soon realized, was that the car was on its side in a ditch. Terry was screaming, but all Jason could attend to was the burning in his chest; it was as if some blazing creature were now astride him, pinning back his arms, holding a staff of fire to his lungs, heart, and spine.

He fought back with a strength no one would have predicted. Another man might have given up, but Jason threw that fiery monster off his chest with such force that sparks streamed into the woods. By the time he got himself and Terry out of the wrecked car, the tall grass along the road was on fire and they had to run all the way to the parkway to flag down a passing car for help.

Jason had only two broken ribs that time, but there was a mark on his chest that resembled a hand. In a few days the imprint faded to the puckered red shadow of any common burn; only a faint impression had been left behind. All the same, he broke up with Terry. She was bad luck when you came right down to it; in his opinion, most women were. They cried and they wanted things from you; they just wouldn't leave you alone. There were times when he sat in his very own house, with his mother and sister and cousin, and he wasn't able to understand them; they spoke a distinctly different language, one he couldn't even begin to fathom, one he certainly didn't want to hear.

That autumn, Jason took to staying away, for a night at

first, then for days at a time. He crashed with friends, and when they'd had enough of him, he invited himself to stay with acquaintances. Finally, he had nowhere to go but the drug houses up beyond the turnpike, where anyone with a little cash and a taste for ruin was welcome. He stopped going to work because he didn't want to deal with Terry and all her needs. He could no longer face his mother, because she continued to gaze at him as though he were the same boy he once was. He wasn't that person anymore, not in any way, shape, or form; he could barely remember what he had once believed in or cared about. He dreamed of oblivion and angels, and he couldn't even bring himself to eat a decent breakfast. Weight fell off his frame and his gums began to bleed; people who'd known him since he was a child avoided him now, hurrying past any corner where he was stationed to beg for a loan or a little spare change. He never went home unless he needed money, and then only after dark, when no one would catch him rifling through drawers for jewelry and cash.

One cloudy November night he came upon Gretel in the kitchen, positioned near the door, as if she'd known he was on his way. He was so strung out he didn't have the sense to be embarrassed when he was discovered creeping around in the middle of the night, climbing in through the window above the sink, since he had long ago lost the key to the front door. Though the temperature was dropping and frost was on the lawns, Jason only wore jeans and a black T-shirt and he was shivering badly. He'd sold his leather coat for a quick fifty bucks, but the truth was, he hadn't even noticed that ice was collecting on the streets or that the palms of his hands had already turned blue.

That night Jason actually talked Gretel into giving him some cash; he was going straight, he told her, he was pulling his life together, but he could see she didn't believe a word. She stared at him as though she could see the faint outline of the burn on his chest, right through his shirt. She wanted to ask him why he was doing this to himself, but instead she bit her lip; he was clueless when it came to disaster and denial, and he always had been.

Gretel walked him out to the front porch. She felt she might never see her brother again, or if she did, she might not recognize him; she could pass him right by, as though the world he now inhabited existed on another plane, one entirely unseen by those who still lived their everyday lives of work and sleep, milk and butter, obligation and concern. The temperature was near freezing and a ring around the moon signaled snow before morning. Gretel considered giving her brother her own leather jacket, but she knew that if she did, it would only be a matter of hours before it was sold.

"It's going to happen," she told Jason. "If you don't watch out."

"Not to me," Jason said. "You're such a worrywart, Gret." As he leaned over to hug her, he had the strangest sensation, almost as though he had left his body to watch himself embrace his sister. "Nothing will happen to me," he vowed. "You wait and see."

But Gretel couldn't even see him once he'd walked down the driveway. Not that she was surprised. It was amazing how quickly someone could disappear into the night when he had a craving for destruction and a few dollars in his pocket. Since Jason didn't have money for his own car and no one with any common sense would lend him one, he walked three miles in order to score, even though snow had already begun to fall. Halfway there, he felt he was being followed, but when he turned, the street was empty. He went on, though the mark on his chest had begun to burn. As he neared the turnpike, the shirt he'd been wearing for days suddenly darkened, as though it had been singed, and then, without warning, the fabric ig nited. There on the sidewalk in front of houses where families were safely asleep in their beds, Jason tore the shirt from his body. It burned down to ash on the asphalt and left nothing but fiery dust. By then, Jason was broiling and freezing at the very same time, and he felt true fear. Clearly, a warning had been tossed down before him on the dark and empty street. All the same, he stared up at Pegasus, which was now in the western corner of the sky.

"You can't stop me," he said.

Jason's words went upward into the icy night and disappeared, swallowed by the cold. He went on, half naked, so spent and exhausted he collapsed when he reached his destination—a basement apartment he knew of where a man could buy just about anything, from heroin to a clean shirt; here, Jason could crash for a while, as long as the money held out.

The apartment was exactly what he thought he'd wanted; there was no longer anyone to tell him how to live and what to do. But each time he got high the fiery creature appeared again, back to torment him. Time after time, he had to fight for his life just to return to that basement, where mattresses were strewn about and no one ever discussed the future. After a while, he began to spy the creature even in the first moments of the day, when he was completely sober and straight.

Did you see that? he'd say to whoever else was hanging out, as though he were a madman who needed validation from any passing junkie. The basement's other inhabitants stared at him with contempt, and even worse, with pity. Couldn't anyone tell that sparks had scorched his eyelashes and his hair? When he removed his boots he often discovered a phosphorous element inside, which glowed with a faint yellow light. The air around him was brutal and hot. Were they blind to all this? Were they too far gone to see? *Seriously,* he'd ask anyone close enough to listen. *Did you feel that?*

Sure, buddy, people would answer, to humor him or simply to get him off their backs. *We feel it.*

When it came down to it, Jason didn't care what they all thought or what they believed. He knew the truth: Something was waiting for him. At night he peered out the window to look upward; even in this dank apartment, he could read his fate in the stars. Still he fought; if anyone came up behind him, he was likely to strike out from pure instinct. He had a wild countenance, that of a man who can find neither courage nor rest; he made certain to lock every window and door. He stopped sleeping, because the creature was there in his dreams, sitting on his chest, aflame with incredible light; on the occasions when he dozed off, he'd awaken to find a thin layer of soot on his skin.

The weather had turned even colder, and Jason had developed a terrible cough. All the same, when his money was gone and he had borrowed and begged far too much, they threw him out of the basement. It was a dreadful night, with ice on the roads inches deep and a gray unforgiving sky, but Jason really wasn't concerned. He'd been pilfering heroin from his host, and he had more than enough to get him through the night. He went down by the parkway, then kept on walking, to the stretch of woods that was still forest, where a man could find some privacy. But his destination was so far and he was so tired he stopped to rest beneath an overpass. He got high right there, like the abandoned souls he and his friends used to laugh about back in high school. He knew he was alone and desperate, but he didn't care. The world had retreated into a single action, getting high, the nadir of all misery and desire.

Jason lay down, his head resting against the tunnel. He was shivering so badly that his head banged against the concrete and he bit his own lips. His fingers and toes were numb and his stomach ached, as though he had consumed nothing but ice and stones. He waited, ready to fight, certain the thing that had been following him would come. But this time when he felt the creature upon him, Jason was grateful for the warmth. The cold he'd experienced was truly horrible, and it was a relief to encounter so much heat. There were flames around his elbows and his ankles which could melt anything: ice and flesh, bone and blood. Despite the sulfur and the ash, Jason embraced his enemy, and as soon as he did he discovered that its appearance mirrored his own: the same blue eyes, the very same smile. He could still see the constellations, even though his eyes were closed; he could see farther than he'd ever imagined possible. He'd thought he was lost, but now he recognized that eternity was all around him, like salt from a shaker or stars in the sky.

Examining the Evidence

The evening was clear, without storm clouds or thunder or any sign of rain, but when Margot Molinaro looked out her kitchen window, she noticed that a glowing object the size of a billiard ball was traveling along the metal fence in her backyard, moving more and more swiftly as it gathered momentum, throwing off sparks that flew out in every direction. Margot barely had time to move away from the window before the thing leapt into her house uninvited, stinking like sulfur and stopping the hands on the clock above the sink. The electromagnetic field inside the house went berserk; wires popped within the walls and every fuse blew.

As Margot watched, shoeless and completely surprised, the ball of lightning moved about the room at only a few inches above the floor, slowly, almost thoughtfully, as though searching for something it couldn't seem to find. The lightning drew nearer and nearer to Margot's bare feet; she closed her eyes, expecting to be burned alive, but the glowing ball suddenly veered away, then picked up speed, and with a whoosh, it hit the refrigerator. The lightning collapsed in a sputtering gasp, like a pan of overcooked rice, falling onto the vinyl tiles, where it left a gaping blue-black mark which sizzled like melted tar.

This strange and luminous phenomenon, which was reported the following day in all the local papers, along with a photograph of Margot looking puzzled and pale, had done as much damage as a small, contained hurricane. Margot had never been a good housekeeper, but now her place was such a disaster that she sat down and cried in the dark, a true necessity as the electricity was no longer working. When she'd pulled herself together, and had washed her face with bottled water—the electromagnetic force had also rattled the pipes, allowing only rusty water to come out of the tap—Margot lit a candle and made a list of things she now must do:

Repaint over the singe marks on the kitchen walls.

Hire an electrician.

Find a plumber.

Figure out why things such as this only happened to her, when every other house on the block was perfectly fine and everyone else in the neighborhood had experienced nothing more unusual than dusky twilight and the call of the warblers, who sang at the very same hour each day.

The following morning, Margot went down to the hardware store and bought a gallon of yellow paint and a box of self-adhesive tiles for the kitchen, then headed over to scan the message board beside the door in search of a half-decent handyman whose services she could afford. Probably the best she could do was Johnny Rickets, who was well known in the neighborhood for his shoddy welding and even worse wiring, but as she took Johnny's card from the board, the owner of the hardware store approached. Like everyone else in town, Mike Sutton had heard about the ball of lightning, and he was eager to see its effects. He took Johnny's card from Margot's hand and ripped it in two.

"Don't hire that crook," he told her. "Hire me."

Mike showed up the following morning at seven, while Margot was out in the backyard boiling water for coffee on the barbecue, since the electric stove was on the blink. When Mike saw the devastation in her house, he was truly impressed. He accepted the cup of Sanka Margot offered, then went to examine the black marks on the wall. "These were some abnormally powerful electrical currents. I'll bet your radio doesn't work."

"Nothing works," Margot said. "Take a look at this."

She picked up a corner of the throw rug she'd borrowed from her cousin Franny, to reveal the tarlike consistency of the vinyl tiles.

Mike knelt to study the floor. "Must have been a geomagnetic storm." Although he had inherited the hardware business from his father, Mike was much more interested in science, and most especially in the stars. People in town would see him on the roof of the store on summer nights, so intent on his telescope he didn't notice when anyone waved or called out his name.

Margot spent the next few days painting and tearing up her old kitchen floor. By then Mike had completed the rewiring and fixed the sink; he assured Margot the mess was far easier to repair than it had looked to be, and he'd send her the bill in the mail. He must have fiddled with the radio and the refrigerator as well, because they were operating perfectly now, as was the stove. All the rest of that week, Margot cursed her fate as she put down her new kitchen floor. Her cousin Franny often came over in the afternoons, to keep Margot company; she'd pull off the paper backing on the tiles and carefully hand them over to Margot, even though she should have been home in bed. Franny had had the worst luck in the world, and although Margot had had the second-worst luck, it was difficult to complain in Franny's presence.

"So how much did all this cost you?" Franny asked, for in fact when the floor was finished the kitchen looked far better than it had before lightning struck.

"I don't know exactly. I haven't gotten the bill yet."

Margot poured them both iced tea. She didn't say a word when Franny took out a cigarette. They both knew that Franny's prognosis was terminal; certainly, after all she'd been through, she had the right to enjoy the time she had left.

Franny breathed out smoke and thought this over. "Mike Sutton did all this work and he didn't send a bill?"

Unless Margot was mistaken, her cousin was actually smiling.

"Don't worry. He'll send one."

But before he could, Margot had to call him back. This time she awoke on an ordinary Tuesday to find that her yard was covered with an odd gossamer netting. When she opened her back door she saw that the wispy stuff was made out of thousands of webs, each a parachute of sorts for a small brown spider. Mike came over that afternoon; he sprayed the lawn and all the shrubbery with a power hose to wash the webs away, but he insisted the spiders were harmless.

"An unusual infestation," he admitted. "Just be thankful it wasn't Japanese beetles."

Margot stood on her back porch to watch Mike collect the last of the webbing, which was drifting from the low branches of a willow tree; she had chills up and down her legs, even though the weather was fine. When Mike started loading up his truck, she followed him out to the street.

"Has this happened to anyone else?" she asked.

"No. Not in this neighborhood. But think of it this way: You probably won't have any mosquitoes this summer."

Did you get the bill yet?" Franny asked the following week. Margot was working in the garden and Franny was lying on the chaise, covered by a wool blanket even though the day was unusually warm. Franny wore a hat and gloves, and shivered whenever a cloud drifted over the sun.

"Don't worry, I'll get charged," Margot assured her cousin.

Margot had on a sleeveless white shirt and a pair of old shorts; her hands and legs were patchy with dirt. She was still pretty, even without her makeup, but what good would that do her? She used to care about her appearance, she used to be wild with hope, but now she worried too much. So far she had found close to a dozen brown spiders in her perennial bed and the soil felt odd to the touch. She dusted herself off, then came to sit on the edge of the chaise, placing Franny's feet in her lap. "Maybe there's a blight on this house. Maybe it was built over an ancient graveyard."

"It was built over a potato farm," Franny reminded her.

"I don't know." Margot sighed. "Things come in threes."

"You had lightning and insects. What comes next?"

They looked at each other and considered. "Floods," they agreed.

To see if there was any way to work against her fate, Margot went down to the basement and turned off the water pressure. She emptied the bins of ice in her freezer and called to cancel her usual delivery of spring water. All the same, she awoke one night with a strange feeling in the pit of her stomach. There was a clatter above her, as if stones were being thrown at her windows and walls. Her heart began to race, as though she were under attack. It was a warm spring night and the crickets were calling. Margot peered out her bedroom window; the neighborhood was peaceful and dark, but her own lawn and walkway seemed oddly shiny and bright. When she looked more closely, she saw that her property was covered with hailstones the size of eggs. The hail had torn through her roof and collected in piles in the attic; by morning the melting hail had leaked through the ceilings, leaving inches of water on the floor.

Mike arrived while Margot was mopping up the living room. She had preserved one hailstone in the freezer, carefully packaged in plastic wrap, so no one would dare call her a liar. The hailstone weighed four ounces and had a dark blue center. Mike looked it over thoughtfully, and while he did, Margot took a step backward; she had a rattling feeling in her chest, almost as if the hailstones were still falling.

"There must have been an atmospheric disturbance right above your house," Mike Sutton said. "A small, distinct field of concentration."

When he went up to patch the roof, Margot fetched the pot of split pea soup she had made earlier, and walked around the corner to Franny's. Margot had brought over dinner for the past few nights, and now her cousin Gretel met her at the side door.

"I don't know why you do this," Gretel said. "She's not eating anymore."

Gretel had spent the past year caring for her mother, but now a nurse had been hired to assist her in the evenings. Still, Gretel only left her mother to go outside and smoke a cigarette or to cry. She didn't care about lightning or hail, and she cared even less about soup, but Margot kissed her anyway and took the soup inside. She ladled out a bowl for herself and one for Franny, then brought a tray into the darkened bedroom.

"It's okay," she told the nurse, who had risen from the rocking chair to help out. "I can manage. Why don't you get yourself some dinner."

No one but the nurse would ever eat the split pea soup, but that didn't matter. Sometimes things happened for which there was no rational explanation and the best anyone could do was record and remember.

"Did you have the flood?" Franny asked when Margot came to lie down beside her in bed.

Margot crawled under the covers and took Franny's hand. "It was hail. It came through the roof, then melted."

Franny laughed. "That was tricky." Her laughter was sweet and thin, like a blade of grass found in the backyard. "That was a good one."

"So what do you think?" Margot said. She was crying, but she tilted her head so that Franny wouldn't see.

"You know what I think," Franny said. "It all adds up."

They held hands until Franny fell asleep. By the time Margot walked home, the sky was already darkening. Dusk fell onto the asphalt like a curtain or a dream, then spread over hedges and lawns. All the same, as soon as Margot turned the corner she could see Mike up on her roof, and try as she might, she couldn't think of a single reason not to run home.

Devotion

That year the month of July was so beautiful people became lazy and stopped going to work. They sat out in their backyards, amazed by the heat and the blue sky; they wept at the sight of sunflowers and hollyhocks. It was a time when even the greediest and most self-centered felt lucky to be alive, and paused to appreciate the sheen of the poplar trees at twilight or the call of the crickets, which lulled small children to sleep. People ate their suppers set out on picnic tables, dreamily passing around cups of lemonade and fresh corn on the cob; they napped on front lawns, dizzy with sunlight and the sound of bees.

There were some people, however, who experienced July not in their own backyards but from behind a wall of glass. Yet even from the vantage point of the hospital windows, Frances Samuelson could see that the clouds resembled sheep and the roses had enjoyed an especially good growing season. Three years earlier, the doctors had advised Franny to get her affairs in order and had given her six months to live. She had lost her breasts and her hair, she had lost both a husband and a son, but she had proven the doctors wrong, until now. Her oncologist, Jack Lerner, felt it wouldn't be long—the cancer had spread to her spine and her brain and she had begun to collapse, her back riddled with pain. Franny, however, knew she was approaching the end of her life because her connection with the world had somehow altered. Objects were not as defined or as singular as they once had been. An apple was as beautiful as a kiss. Her daughter's face was no different from the moon. There were times when Franny could peer right through the present and see layers of the past: She could drink a glass of cool water fetched from her own kitchen sink and at the very same time be a baby rocked in her carriage. She could cry out in pain and still be a young woman choosing her wedding dress or a mother whose child has taken a first step.

She stayed at home for as long as she could, but when her strength was gone, when she was too weak even to worry if her sweet daughter Gretel would inherit her fate or if her beloved cousin Margot would have to continue to sleep on the floor beside her bed, Dr. Lerner suggested she come to the hospital, and Franny agreed. She had always been a woman who took care of details; she wouldn't think of going out of town without leaving an itemized note for the paperboy. Now, she didn't even collect her toothbrush and nightgown; she let them take her by wheelchair, relieved that she could close her eyes and rest. She had become too weak to get to the bathroom on her own or speak a full sentence, but she had been taking care of other people for so long it was difficult to give it all up. How odd to be drifting into this realm where she had no control, where a sob was not so very different from a smile. She had never in her life believed in medication and had rarely taken an aspirin, but now she was attached to a morphine pump, as was the woman in the bed next to hers. But that was a bit of good fortune: at least they were in this together.

"She thinks there's another patient in this room," she heard Margot tell the oncologist, clearly convinced that levelheaded Franny had taken to hallucinating.

"She deserves to see whatever she wants to see," Lerner said. He was the sort of doctor who held his patient's hand when he had to deliver bad news, and wept in his car while he drove home. After all these years, he still wasn't certain whether the forces above were working with or against him, but he'd seen enough miracles and agony to convince him that anything was possible.

The patient in the bed next to Franny's was beautiful,

although she barely moved and spoke only when there were no visitors or nurses in the room. She had no hair and her eyes were cloudy; she gave off the scent of roses and grass.

Breathe in, she'd whisper to Franny late at night, when the lights in the hospital parking lot filtered through the windows and everything seemed shiny, as though thousands of fireflies clung to the glass. *Breathe out,* she'd remind her.

Gretel and Margot took turns staying with Franny. They opened the curtains so that the shadows shifted; they brought flowers in a vase. They loved her so much Franny could feel it; their love was as palpable as a table or a chair, it was as real as a bandage or a piece of pie. But although Franny loved them in return, she could also feel their grief, and such things were a burden to her now, tying her not only to those who loved her but to her own pain. What she longed for most were the hours when she and the woman in the next bed were alone.

Look at what you have, the woman would tell her, and sure enough, Franny could see the stars, not through the window but there in the palm of her own hand.

When the levels of morphine rose to keep pace with the level of her pain, Franny began to dream that she was a little girl on a perfect July day. The scent of fresh grass was delicious. The roses were bigger than cabbages. Everything was out in front of her, the world stretched on and on. Sometimes Margot would be with her in her dreams, just as she had always been when they were girls. Frick and Frack, people would call them. Me and Too, the inseparable pair.

They'd run down hill after hill until they were breathless, convulsed with giggles. Margot was always the fastest, but even when she was first, she'd wait for her cousin.

"Go on," Franny told her. She opened her eyes and there was Margot, beside her in a hard-backed chair, sobbing. "You don't have to wait for me." Her voice was so distant that Margot had to bend close; still it was difficult to hear. "Go and don't feel guilty."

By now, Franny had lost her vision; she could only see shadows. She heard pieces of conversation, but could not recognize certain words: darling, dusk, ashes, pear, they had all become one, a single band of light. Things of this world fell away from her: she could no longer sense the pressure of an IV needle in her tired vein, but the coo of a dove a hundred miles away reverberated inside her ear. She knew that Dr. Lerner sometimes came into her room and cried when he thought she was sleeping. She knew that Gretel sat beside her for hours, watching her breathe, refusing to go home, as if pure will and devotion could keep her mother alive.

But in fact, Franny no longer minded when her visitors left her. After the nurses had gone down the hall to fill out their daily charts and those who loved her had journeyed to the cafeteria to gulp mugs of black coffee, the air in the room became lighter, as though the clouds had drifted in through the windows. The bed of the woman next to her had been pushed closer. They could hold hands now, palm to palm, fingertip to fingertip. Intertwined, their hands were equally beautiful and pale.

Franny was happy to gaze into the woman's cloudy eyes; she was grateful for the scent of roses. In the midst of her terrible pain, she was reminded of all she had to be thankful for, but there were times when that only served to make her hold on more tightly. Her fingers ached from holding on that way; her breath rattled, hard, nearly cracking her ribs with the strain.

All we have to do is let go, the woman told Franny.

Right in front of them Franny could spy a lake where little fish swam in the shallows. There was a park beyond the lake, in which a maze had been fashioned out of hedges. Franny was afraid of thorns; still, she went closer. The other woman was already there, reaching out her hand, fearless as always. But as it happened, there were no thorns to draw blood, only green leaves and the red roses Franny's very own daughter had planted beside their house. Franny could hear women crying, but there was no difference between that sound and the echo of the wind, so she went a little farther. Now she saw there was a door in the hedge, one that was nearly invisible to the naked eye. Franny turned to gaze at the beautiful woman beside her. She could hear the ticking of the clock in her hospital room and the beat of her own heart, slow as deep water. No one who had come this far needed to hesitate or look backward, and because she had always known this to be true, she stepped through the gate.

Still Among the Living

Margot Molinaro Sutton was the only person waiting at the arrivals gate at the Fort Lauderdale airport who didn't have white hair. She was there to meet her cousin Gretel, whom she loved like a daughter. True, there were only fifteen years between them, but those years were enough to mark a generation, and now that Gretel's mother was gone Margot had taken it upon herself to watch over her cousin, especially during vacations. Not that Gretel was the sort of person who might actually enjoy herself, on vacation or otherwise. It was ninety-two degrees in South Florida, but when Gretel walked off the plane she was wearing the same black wool dress she'd worn to her mother's funeral.

"You've got to be kidding," Margot said after she hugged Gretel. "Wool? In this climate?"

She grabbed Gretel's overnight case, but Gretel snatched it right back. "I've got it," Gretel insisted.

You had to be that way with Margot, or she'd just take over. She was good-hearted in the worst way. Let down your guard for a minute, and kaboom, she'd have your whole life rearranged. Gretel's life was running exactly the way she wanted it to, thank you very much. She had just finished her first year at NYU and had come down to visit Margot before summer school started. Gretel was always in a hurry to finish things, and now that she'd arrived in Fort Lauderdale, she was ready to turn around and go back to school.

"It's so hot," she said when they walked out of the terminal and the temperature slapped her in the face. She could practically feel the little black wool dress shrinking on her body.

"It's Florida," Margot reminded her. "What did you expect? Igloos? Don't tell me you're actually wearing panty hose. Are you nuts? Have you ever heard of shorts?"

Gretel laughed as she got into her cousin's car. Margot had driven her first husband's Mustang until it died of terminal engine seizure, and now her new husband, Mike Sutton, who had opened a chain of hardware stores all across South Florida, had bought her the car of her dreams. A Corvette.

"Amazing," Gretel said. "You really did it."

"Did what? Married a man who can make money with his eyes closed? What an accomplishment." Margot flipped open the glove compartment, where she kept her chiffon scarves. "Take one. You'll need it."

"Admit it," Gretel said. "You found happiness."

They drove the scenic route, along 1A. The ocean was pale green and turquoise. Pelicans glided over the water. All the houses were white and pink and red. Margot could see why someone would believe she'd gotten everything she'd ever wanted. She slipped on her sunglasses. Heat waves rose from the asphalt and the air smelled like orange blossoms.

It was so hot in Florida at this time of year the mosquitoes were too scorched to fly, and landed with thumps on car windshields. As soon as she could, Gretel peeled off her panty hose. Her legs were as white as icicles.

"Holy moly," Margot said. "We're going to have to work on your tan."

Neither of them mentioned Gretel's mother, Frances, although they both missed her like crazy. Instead of discussing cancer or sorrow or the possibility of an afterlife, they went to Margot's favorite junk shop in Delray Beach and bought Gretel a pair of flip-flops, some wraparound sunglasses, suntan lotion, a straw purse, and a bathing suit.

When they got back in the Corvette, Gretel fished around in her shopping bag. "What is this?"

She had chosen a black tank suit, but somehow a pink bikini had wound up among her purchases.

"Don't be mad," Margot pleaded.

"I'm not wearing this." Gretel tossed the bikini back in the bag. All the same, she couldn't help but notice the fabric was the same exact shade as the palest climbing roses. The tint of seashells on a deserted beach, or the mouth of someone you might want to kiss.

That night, dinner was served out by the pool. They flopped into lounge chairs with glasses of chilled white wine, and watched Mike barbecue. He was fixing skewers of halibut, red pepper, and shrimp with a red wine and tarragon marinade he'd invented himself.

"Don't tell me I have everything," Margot said.

"Okay." Gretel closed her eyes and breathed in the scent of the jasmine growing along the fence. "I won't tell you."

"But that doesn't mean I won't sometime real soon," Margot informed her cousin.

Gretel opened one eye and smiled. This sounded like one of Margot's plans. She came up with them all the time. She was the one to decide she and Gretel's mother should go into the catering business together, which had kept them both afloat for years. She had told Mike that the wave of the future was a chain of stores, rather than just one, and look at the success he had made. When Margot had something in mind, look out; she wasn't about to sit still.

They left in the morning, as soon as Mike had gone to work.

"I'll be waiting for you, sweetie," Margot had whispered to Mike when she kissed him goodbye, but she'd already been holding the keys to the Corvette in her hand.

"He's the best," she told Gretel as they headed north on the interstate.

Gretel was still wearing her black dress, but she'd taken a pair of scissors to the wool and scooped out the neck in deference to the weather. She'd slipped on the yellow flip-flops she'd bought the day before, and left her heavy black shoes under the bed in Margot's guest room. She had one of Margot's scarves tied around her hair; it was frothy and blue, the exact color of the Florida sky. Gretel flipped down the visor and smiled when she caught sight of herself, a vision in chiffon and sunglasses.

"When my neighbor Dora told me about this woman, I thought I'd wait for you to go with me," Margot said.

"Yeah, sure." Gretel smirked. "Meaning you were afraid to go yourself."

"I'm not afraid." But in truth, Margot had been awake all night, her nerves a jumbled mess.

"Fine. We'll go and you'll see it's bullshit and that will be that."

The woman in question was located in a shopping mall in Glades, beside the Dunkin' Donuts. Her name was Natalie LeFrance, and she could cure whatever afflicted you for a hundred and fifty dollars, or so Margot's neighbor Dora had sworn. Dora herself had been covered with warts until her visit to Glades and now her skin was clear and smooth. Well, Margot's problem was more serious than warts, so naturally she was a little anxious. She had the right to be.

What Margot wanted was a baby. She had yearned for

one for more than sixteen years, all through her first marriage, and during those years when she was single, and now, with Mike. Every doctor she went to told her pregnancy was impossible for her, she'd have to be a fool to keep trying. She'd read all the medical literature about infertility, been to the specialists, and had followed any suggestions, no matter how far-fetched. She had stood on her head directly after sex. She'd eaten only chocolate and asparagus, then switched to a diet of grapefruit and hard-boiled eggs. She'd had intercourse once a month, then three times a day, and none of it had worked. Now here she was, in a parking lot, pulling into a space next to a Fotomat on a broiling-hot day. It was a run-down shopping area with weeds sprouting through the asphalt and a big old palm offering the only shade. The air smelled like sugar and doughnuts and melting tar.

"Lovely spot," Gretel said. "It looks like the perfect place to get mugged."

But Margot had a good feeling. She felt light-headed and somehow carefree.

"This is going to work," she insisted. "I just know it."

"Oh, sure. If you believe in it," Gretel said.

"You think it's wrong to believe in something?"

Margot had gotten out her lipstick and had begun to reapply the deep scarlet color to her lips. Now she turned to her cousin, and Margot seemed so innocent and so desperate Gretel didn't have the heart to be honest.

"Fine. If you want to believe you can find a cure in a shopping center, then believe."

Gretel herself had believed in very little since the deaths of her mother and her brother, and who could blame her? Okay, maybe she believed in random atrocities, the old anthill theory, that human beings were equally liable to be squashed by the careless feet of fate.

When Margot and Gretel got out of the car, they noticed that two guys who worked at the Fotomat were leaning out their window, giving the Corvette the once-over.

"Lock it," Gretel said.

"Whatever happens happens." Margot had bigger issues than a possible stolen vehicle. *"C'est la vie."*

"Okay. It's your car." Gretel took the chiffon scarf from her head, then tied it around her throat so that she gave a far jauntier appearance than she meant to. "But let me ask you one thing. Do you really think someone with true healing powers would be located next to a Dunkin' Donuts?"

"Depends on the rents." Margot knocked three times on the door, as per Dora's recommendation, then rang the bell twice. She'd wanted this baby for so long it had almost become a living, breathing person already.

"Tell me one thing." Gretel took off her sunglasses in spite of the Florida glare. "Do you think she could have helped my mother?"

Gretel's mother's cancer had metastasized so quickly and so aggressively it was like a kick from the center of the universe that struck and destroyed before anyone had time to blink.

"I don't know," Margot admitted. "Maybe. Maybe not."

Gretel's black dress was sticking to her skin like needles and pins. Margot had recognized it as the one Gretel had worn to her mother's funeral the minute her cousin had stepped off the plane, but she was far too polite to mention her observation. Gretel had been wearing the dress almost constantly for over a year. She'd been washing it by hand, but it was shrinking all the same.

"If we'd just taken my mother here, she'd still be alive? Is that what you're trying to tell me?"

For years Gretel had been cutting her own hair and the dark strands stuck up in wisps all over her head. This hairstyle looked like the saddest thing in the world to Margot. She remembered the day Gretel was born, all the hope she and Frances had had, and now Gretel was a full-grown woman with a terrible haircut who didn't believe in anything.

"Honey, we did everything we could for your mother."

"Maybe we didn't," Gretel said. Her voice sounded funny, even to herself. The black dress felt like a nest of hornets on her back.

Gretel sat down on the curb, where weeds with yellow flowers were growing. She started to sneeze and her eyes welled up, but she didn't care.

Margot sat down beside her cousin. "We did everything," she said. "Trust me."

They had been buzzed into the storefront, but they hadn't noticed. Now the door opened and a woman wearing short shorts and a white halter top appeared.

"Are you coming in or not?" It was Natalie LeFrance, the healer. Margot recognized her from the neighbor's description. Thick hair pulled into a ponytail. Silver earrings. A little blue tattoo at the base of her neck in the shape of a spider, caught in a web.

"What do you think?" Margot asked Gretel. "Should we?"

Gretel could not remember the last time her cousin had asked for her advice. "We're here." Gretel shrugged. "What the hell."

The storefront was air-conditioned and as cold as a freezer. There were bottles of herbs on a shelf, along with a TV, turned on without the sound. They sat around a table and drank glasses of warm ginger ale.

"I can see you're in a lot of pain," Natalie said to Gretel.

"I'm not the client," Gretel informed her. She couldn't help the smirk on her face.

"Really? I'm seeing pain."

"I'm the one with the problem." Margot tapped on the table. "I can't get pregnant."

"Okay. Listen to me. I want you to have sex with your husband twice tonight. Once in the moonlight, once in the dark." Natalie LeFrance leaned both elbows on the table and lowered her voice confidentially, even though the closest human life-forms were the Fotomat guys out in the parking lot. "You understand, of course, I have to be paid for my services."

Gretel snorted. "Naturally."

Margot reached for her purse to search for the

hundred and fifty dollars she had brought along, but the healer stopped her.

"Not money. The ring."

Margot's diamond was just under two carats, an unusual yellow-white stone.

"Oh, yeah, right." Gretel got a good laugh out of this one. "Like she'd give you her ring."

The odd thing was, the ring had always fit Margot's finger perfectly, but now it felt too heavy. All at once, she realized how much more comfortable she would feel without it. She slipped it off.

"You're crazy," Gretel said.

The healer had the diamond in her pocket before you could count to three. "Right before you have sex, eat this." She took Margot's hand and dropped a large avocado into her palm. Next she gave Margot a packet of herbs. "Mix this in—every bit of it."

Margot nodded. She actually had tears in her eyes, that's how close she felt to her heart's desire. When they went back outside, the heat was like a brick wall. The parking lot seemed to be melting. The two guys from the Fotomat had been sitting in the Corvette, but as soon as they caught sight of Margot and Gretel approaching, they scrambled out.

After she'd gotten into the car, Gretel locked her door and rolled up her window. "A diamond ring in exchange for an avocado and some catnip," she scoffed. "Now that's a deal."

"We'll just have to see, won't we?" They were pulling

out into traffic, but Margot would have felt safe even if she hadn't looked both ways. That's how secure she was. That's how certain she was that fate would see her through.

"I think Mike and I should have you locked up," Gretel informed her cousin.

"Just try it." Margot grinned. She felt so extremely light she might have been made of pure air. "You won't get far."

They drove at eighty miles an hour the whole way home, and only stopped once, to pick up some groceries. Gretel, so used to cold, gray New York, hadn't bothered with sunscreen, and by the time they got home her cheeks were pink. While Margot fixed supper and waited for Mike, Gretel went upstairs to the guest room. She stretched out, and without meaning to, fell asleep in the heat of the late afternoon. She was so exhausted she might have slept the whole night through, if she hadn't heard them in their bed. Margot and Mike were all the way down the hall, behind the closed doors of their bedroom, but Gretel could still hear them having sex. It was so wild many of the neighborhood cats had gathered on the closest street corner to join in, howling beneath a sliver of silvery moon.

Gretel put on her black dress, and for the sake of privacy, she went downstairs. But even down in the kitchen, she could still hear Mike and Margot making love. She found her way to the patio, where the nearly empty bowl of guacamole Margot had served Mike was left on a wrought-iron table. Still, she could hear them going at it, even outside. At last, she went to the pool, which looked green in the moonlight. There were white moths skimming over the surface of the water and a thousand stars in the sky. At night, the scent of jasmine was sweet and rich and something was calling—a cricket or a frog, Gretel couldn't tell.

She sat at the shallow end of the pool, her legs dangling in the water. Margot and Mike must have opted for an open window rather than air-conditioning, even on this hot night, because Gretel continued to hear them. She had been thinking about sorrow for so long she was amazed to hear the sound of love. What a foreign language it was. How odd to an ear unused to such things. Gretel swung her feet back and forth, so that she would hear only the ripple of water, but those echoes of love kept on and on. The woolen dress was driving her mad by now; she could have sworn she had somehow picked up fleas. For two cents she would have ripped it off right then and there; instead, she did something she would have never expected of herself. She dove right into the pool.

The whole world turned fish-cool and silent. When she surfaced and began to swim laps, all she heard was water. So much liquid was an extreme relief; soon she began to shiver, not with cold but with pure pleasure. She felt as though she'd been wandering in the desert for a thousand years, and was thirsty enough to drink an entire ocean. She didn't go back into the house until long past midnight, and by then it was quiet. She left circles of chlorinated water on the tile floors and on the stairs. The dress had shrunk so badly it no longer reached past her thighs. It was so tight she had to cut it off with a pair of manicure scissors she found in the medicine cabinet.

In the morning, when Margot came down to fix coffee, Gretel was already out by the pool.

"How did it go?" Gretel called when she heard the commotion in the kitchen. She was wearing the pink bikini she never thought she'd have a need for.

"Great," Margot called back.

Margot had already decided that if the baby was a girl she'd name her Francesca. If a boy, he'd be Frankie. And if it was neither, why, then she'd go and buy herself another diamond ring—three carats and flawless.

Margot took the orange juice from the fridge, poured two glassfuls, then carried them out to the patio. "Hey," she said when she spied Gretel without the horrible black dress. She stopped in her tracks. "What happened to you?"

"Don't get all excited." Margot could read too much into anything. "I just went for a swim."

Margot placed the glasses of juice on the little metal table. "If I added a little champagne to the OJ, we'd have ourselves mimosas."

Gretel slipped on her sunglasses while she waited for Margot to collect the bottle of champagne Mike had opened last night. The hour was so early even the birds were still in the process of waking. All the same, it was clearly going to be an incredible day; you could tell that from the way the sun was rising.

"It's flat but it's good," Margot said when she returned to fix their mimosas. "Just like me."

"Promise you won't ever tell me I have everything." In spite of herself, Gretel noticed the sky was breaking open above them into delirious shades of blue. "Swear that you won't."

"All right," Margot agreed. "I won't tell you."

Local Girls

Gretel stands by the gate, her fingers wrapped around the metal fence post. There are the roses, which she planted herself. Once, they were nothing more than seedlings packaged in brown paper and string, but with time they've become a gorgeous torrent of blooms, tumbling over the fence. Where the cherry tree had been, there is now a bed of English ivy, the growth so dense and thick anyone would guess it had been there forever. The sky is terrifically blue and clear; it's the only thing which has remained constant. Those clouds have always turned to castles when you squint your eyes, but once you blink, they're gone. Blink again, and you'll come to believe you never even saw them in the first place. It was all your imagination, that's what you'll start to think; it was all in your mind.

Today the weather is hot, a June day close to perfection. Bees are hovering above the lawn; Gretel can hear them, in spite of the noise echoing from the Southern State Parkway. She sits cross-legged on the grass, although this is no longer her house and hasn't been for some time, nearly five years. She leans down and listens to the droning of bees and she can't help but wonder why she never heard them during all those years when she lived here. Maybe she wasn't paying attention, but she's paying attention now. There's Jill, Gretel's oldest friend in the world, walking down the street. Gretel can divine Jill's presence intuitively; she knows the slap of Jill's clogs on the cement and the bone-chilling squeak Jill's son Leonardo manages to summon forth when he rides his bicycle.

"What are you doing over there?" Jill calls.

Gretel waves from the lawn, then shades her eyes against the sun so she can see her childhood friend more clearly. There Jill is, at the edge of the driveway, with her three children: Leonardo, aged seven; Eddie junior, who's called Doc; and the baby, Angela, who at eleven months is already walking. Jill's blond hair is pulled into a ponytail; even after three pregnancies, she still has the legs to wear short shorts. Now she plops the baby down on the lawn and marches over to Gretel.

"Are you crazy? We hate these people." She nods to Gretel's old house. "Nobody in the neighborhood talks to them. Get up." She gives Gretel a little kick in the shin to prove her point. "Move it."

"Ow," Gretel says, but she moves it all the same.

"They're a horrible family." Jill heads for Angela, who is tearing leaves from an ornamental shrub. "If they see us on their property, they'll call the police. Pigs," she calls over her shoulder. "They never come to the block party," she tells Gretel. "But then again, neither did you."

"There used to be block parties?" Gretel asks.

Jill shakes her head when she considers what a pathetic specimen Gretel was, and perhaps still is, in spite of her degree from NYU and the five years she's spent in Manhattan. "Every August," she informs Gretel, who clearly still has her head in the clouds. "My mother always made macaroni salad. Your mother was always working."

Gretel and Jill have looped arms; they're following Jill's kids down the street to the Harringtons' house, Jill's house now, since her parents have moved to a condo in Fort Lauderdale, allowing Jill and her husband to take over the mortgage.

"We'll still be paying it off from our graves," Jill has cheerfully told Gretel, not that she has to tell anyone that Eddie is not exactly a financial genius. Luckily, the LoPaccas have taken him into the family business, and he's got his own delivery route, way out on the Island. His sister, Terry, is the real heir apparent, and runs the LoPaccas' bread factory.

"Terry has a shrine to your brother set up in her bedroom," Jill tells Gretel as they follow the kids along.

"Still? You'd think she'd be over him."

"Jason's like a saint in her eyes. I think she's forgotten anything negative. I pity her husband."

"She got married?" Gretel asks. Everyone's doing it, it seems. Except for her.

"Hey!" Jill suddenly stops, hands on her hips. "What do you think you're doing?" she asks Leonardo, her oldest, who has just narrowly escaped being hit by a car.

"Nothing," he answers.

"You'd better watch where you're going," she tells her son. "No driver's going to watch out for you."

Gretel feels so dreamy being back here in June. It was always her favorite time of the year, this glorious, untrustworthy month when anything seems possible. Here they are at Jill's house, a destination Gretel has reached a million times before. She takes a good look now and realizes how small the house is, how impossibly green the grass seems to be.

"Is this real?" Gretel leans over and pulls out a handful of turf.

"Yes, it's real," Jill says. It's never easy to tell whether or not Jill's insulted; she still has a permanent pout. "Eddie works like a dog on this lawn. You're just used to asphalt and cement."

There's a little pool set out in the backyard, just as there was when Jill and Gretel were kids. Back then, Jill's mother was too distracted and depressed to notice much of what they were doing, but Jill watches her children carefully.

"Don't you push your sister," she shouts at Doc as she fills the pool up with the hose. "And don't think I can't see everything you do."

Doc, who's just turned five, sits contritely on the grass. They can all hear Leo's bike out on the street, squeaking and whining as he rides in circles and figure eights. Gretel sprawls in a lawn chair. She used to see this yard from her own bedroom window, but no one in her family lives here anymore. Her mother and brother are dead, her father lives on the North Shore with his second wife, even her cousin Margot moved to Florida, where she lives with her husband and their son, Frankie, a sweet little whirlwind who likes to call Gretel on the phone and tell knock-knock jokes.

Jill has gone into the kitchen for some Kool-Aid and paper cups, and after she returns to give everyone a drink, she throws herself down on the plastic lawn chair beside Gretel's. "Give me the strength to go on," she cries. Jill pulls a pack of cigarettes from her shorts pocket and offers one to Gretel.

"I quit," Gretel informs her friend.

"Seriously? Completely?"

Whenever Jill came into the city, she and Gretel would go to clubs and smoke and drink and complain about their lives, but of course Jill hasn't been into the city since Angela was born, and during that time Gretel has quit a lot of things. She stopped cutting her own hair, for instance, and now pays for it to be styled. She stopped crying in the middle of the night. She stopped feeling that everyone's bad fortune was her responsibility—all right, maybe she feels it occasionally, but whenever she does, she goes out and buys a new pair of earrings, or a blouse she can't afford, and that seems to help. Now she has gone even further: at the base of her wrist is a small blue tattoo—胆—the symbol for courage.

"I can't believe it!" Jill cries. "You went and got that without telling me!" Jill is actually jealous. Of Gretel. Jill's husband, Eddie, would never allow her to have a tattoo. Why, he won't even let her have Angela's ears pierced, even though she would look so cute with little pearl studs. Sure, Jill could sneak Angela over to her cousin Marianne, who pierces ears with a sharp needle right at her kitchen table, but it wouldn't be worth the fight she'd have to have with Eddie. Not that she listens to him. Not really. He never liked her going into the city to see Gretel, to all those crummy apartments, with all those weird roommates, and that never stopped Jill. If Eddie knew the half of it, the ratty clubs they went to, the lunatic roommate who stood out on a window ledge above Fourteenth Street convinced she could fly, he would have gone berserk.

The real reason Jill and Gretel haven't seen each other much in the past two years has nothing to do with Eddie, at least not in that way. It's jealousy, that's the problem; it's coveting something you'd never actually want in real life, but still desire in your dreams, the silliest dreams, the ones you simply can't shake, even now, when you're not a kid anymore and should know better than to traffic in envy. Each wants a bit of the other's life. Not the whole thing of course, not the loneliness or the exhaustion; just the best parts, the prizes.

"Angela is the cutest girl in the world," Gretel decides.

The late afternoon is more scorching than ever, even in Jill's shady backyard. Gretel has been drinking Kool-Aid, which is a great deal sweeter than she had remembered; the kids are all in the pool, making so much noise the sound blends together into one deafening blast. She believes her appraisal of Angela to be unbiased, even though she is the child's godmother.

"I know," Jill agrees. "Especially when she's sleeping."

They can hear Eddie's truck when he pulls into the driveway, sputtering with a defective muffler, and they look at each other and laugh. Eddie always made sure you knew he was around.

"Hey," he shouts when he sees Jill and Gretel. "Great to see you," he tells Gretel as she greets him. He puts his arm around her and pulls her too close. "You have never looked better. Wow."

"Oh, shut up," Jill tells him.

"You shut up," he says, and he leans down to kiss her, a real kiss, as if they were madly in love.

Maybe Jill and Eddie are still crazy about each other, maybe they always have been. Gretel has always had a difficult time understanding why people are drawn to each other, and why they break apart. Still, she knows one thing for certain: Never judge a relationship unless you're the one wrapped up in its arms.

"Terry's coming for dinner," Eddie says as he heads for the house to take a shower.

"Thanks for telling me," Jill shouts after him. "How about some notice next time?" When he turns on the porch to take a bow, Jill laughs in spite of herself. "Idiot," she says warmly.

Gretel can't help but wonder if she's genetically incapable of forming a lasting relationship. Her only real boyfriend in high school was a disaster, and everyone she dated in college was a disappointment of one sort or another. She's here at Jill's for the weekend before heading to California, where Eugene Kessler, an old friend of her brother's who disappeared years ago, has resurfaced to publish a magazine in Menlo Park. Gretel has been hired as associate editor, and Jill is green with envy. At last.

"You'll have an expense account." Lately, Jill gets a shimmery look whenever she talks about Gretel's future. You'd think she was the one who'd soon be returning people's manuscripts and fixing French-roast coffee. "You'll wear really short skirts."

"I don't think so." Although if she did they would all be black—her color.

They're carrying cups and toys into the kitchen, which is broiling-hot. There's a lasagna in the oven, hopefully enough now that Terry and her husband have been added to the dinner table.

"You'll meet somebody in a band the first week you're in California. A guitarist. No, a drummer. They're cuter and they don't have such big egos."

"Dream on." Gretel laughs, but all the same, she's feeling little pinpricks of hope.

By the time the salad is fixed, and the kids' hands washed, Terry and her husband, Tim, who works in the accounting department at the LoPaccas' bakery, have arrived.

"Oh, my God, Gretel, you look terrific." Terry hugs Gretel as if they were once best friends, instead of acquaintances who might or might not smile when they passed each other on the street. "Jason's sister," Terry informs her husband. "It still breaks my heart," she tells Gretel. "Every time I think about what might have been."

When Eddie comes in, his hair wet from the shower, he makes a show of greeting his guests, as though the overcrowded, stifling kitchen really was his castle.

"No lasagna for me," Tim says when Jill is about to serve him. "Just salad."

"You don't like lasagna?" Eddie asks.

"Let me put it this way," Tim says. He has always been a fanatical Beatles fan, and refers to the group to prove any possible point. "I used to be Paul. Now I'm John."

For some reason Gretel laughs out loud, then quickly covers her mouth with her hand.

Eddie stares at his brother-in-law. "What's that supposed to mean?"

"Eddie," Jill warns as she serves Terry, then the kids.

"No, really. Is that supposed to mean something?"

"It means nothing," Terry tells Eddie. "Why are you even listening to him?"

"Who's the walrus?" Tim goads his brother-in-law.

"Am I supposed to be Paul, and you're John because you're a superior being? Is that what you're saying?" Eddie asks Tim.

"Will you just shut up?" Jill says. "Maybe you're Ringo."

"I don't think so." Eddie grins. "No way."

When he smiles, Gretel can see why Jill fell for him in the first place. He definitely has his appeal. Later, as Jill is putting the two youngest kids to bed, and Terry is clearing the table, Eddie comes up behind Gretel while she's washing the dishes.

"Did you ever think all you needed was a really great fuck?" he asks Gretel. He loves to do this, play with her, test her loyalty to Jill.

"You know what I'd really like?" Gretel whispers, her voice low and sweet.

Eddie puts his hands on her waist and moves closer.

"For you to do the pots."

"Hey, baby, it's your loss," Eddie tells her when she tosses him the sopping-wet sponge. "Suffer."

Gretel goes out to the patio, where they'll be having drinks and dessert. There's the smell of grass and of a barbecue in someone else's yard.

"What a moron Eddie is," Terry says as she pours Gretel a glass of wine. It's still light enough so that Terry's husband can toss a ball around with Leonardo, light enough so that Gretel can see tears in Terry's eyes.

"Sorry." Terry wipes at her tears. "I get this way when I think of your brother."

Gretel knows this often happens when someone dies

young, before he's had time to completely disappoint or betray those who love him.

"You wouldn't have been happy with him," Gretel tells Terry, and it's the truth. Her brother, Jason, was too wounded and too pure for anything as simple as happiness. "You would have been miserable."

Out in the grass, Tim throws the ball to Leo, who manages to catch it every single time.

"I've got it!" Leo shouts. "Look at me!"

"I try to tell myself the past is the past. Let it go." Terry wipes her eyes with the back of her hand and pulls herself together.

Gretel stares past the fences which separated her yard from Jill's. It was so long ago when they used to climb out their windows at night. In the summer, everyone else would be fast asleep with their windows wide open or their air conditioners turned on, but not them. They had too much to accomplish; they had their whole lives ahead of them.

"You know what they're calling this street now?" Eddie asks when he comes out with some plastic chairs and a cooler of beer. "Suicide Alley."

"What's suicide?" Leonardo calls from the grass.

"Thank you so much for that lovely addition to his vocabulary," Jill says to Eddie. She's brought out the cheesecake she fixed early that morning, which she cuts into slices and serves on the little rose-patterned plates that her mother always said were too fragile for everyday use.

"Hey, it's life. You want to protect him from everything."

"That's right," Jill says. "I do."

Gretel cracks up, and Jill joins right in.

"Was that funny?" Eddie asks. "Did I miss something?"

"Two girls killed themselves right down the street," Terry informs Gretel. "Was it last week?"

"The last day of May," Jill says. "Easy," she calls to Tim after he pitches a fastball to Leo. "I want him to keep those teeth."

"We had *Newsday* here interviewing everybody, and who do they pick to talk to? Those creeps who bought your old house, Gretel. They said this is an alienating neighborhood. Well, they're definitely alienated now. No one will ever talk to them—not on this block. That's for sure."

"Sounds like they don't care," Gretel says.

Twilight is already falling, like ashes, in wavy purple clouds.

"Everybody cares," Jill says.

That night, in the lower bunk of Leonardo's bed, Gretel can't sleep. It's not the heat, or the sound of Leo grinding his teeth, that keeps her awake. It's the deepness of the night; it's the way her memories won't leave her alone. A long time ago, Gretel set up a tightrope in her backyard, stretching a jump rope between two pine trees. She wore black ballet slippers that her grandmother had given her, and she carried a small paper parasol. She practiced for hours, but she couldn't take a single step on the rope without falling. Once, as she was falling, she looked up to see Jill out in her yard. Through the grid of metal fences, Jill had been watching, but she never mentioned Gretel's failure. In fact, if Gretel remembers correctly, Jill was the one to turn away.

Who will watch her now and not fault her for falling? Who will she call in the middle of the night? Who will talk until there's nothing more to say? Gretel gets out of bed in the dark, silent and careful not to wake Leonardo. She pulls on some shorts, tucks in her T-shirt, and makes her way through the house, navigating with one hand on the wall. When she gets out to the yard she can see her old house, the angles of the roof, the chimney, the ivy. There is her bedroom window. There is the front door. There are the roses, whose scent carries in the thick night air.

It's no surprise to find Jill out on the steps, drinking a cold beer. Jill always had trouble sleeping. Some people said it was a complete and total waste when Jill got pregnant and dropped out of school, and if truth be told, Gretel was one of them. Now, she's not so sure.

"Bad dream?" Jill asks.

Gretel wishes nightmares were all that kept her awake. She cannot tell which disturbs her sleep more, the future or the past.

"It's too hot," she says.

If this were Gretel's last night on earth she would want the moonlight to be like this, spilling out over the lawns.

"Too hot to handle." In the silvery light, Jill looks as young as ever. She hands Gretel a cold beer from the cooler and grins. "I was the pretty one, you were the smart one."

"Screw you," Gretel says. "I was the pretty one."

Jill starts to laugh. "Sorry," she says when Gretel shoots her a look. "I love you anyway. Even if you are smart."

They walk around to the front of the house, barefoot, and although Jill has finished her beer, Gretel brings hers along. They're both tired, but the night is so hot, and by now they know they'll never get to sleep. Gretel has to leave for the airport at five-thirty a.m., so she may as well stay awake and catch a nap on the plane. In only a few hours, she and Jill will cry beside the boarding gate, but now they're sharing Gretel's beer and taking their time, walking slowly, like tourists, even though this is a landscape they know inside out. The streetlamps cast a hazy glow, the light of a dream you're not quite finished waking from. Fireflies drift across the lawns.

"This is the place where the two girls died." Jill points across the street to a house that looks exactly like all the rest. "They killed themselves in the garage."

Gretel wishes now that she'd worn shoes. The concrete retains heat; if anything, it seems to grow hotter at night. "What a way to go."

"They made a secret pact. Their lives were screwed up. Boy problems. Family problems. The same exact troubles we had."

Jill sounds calm, but her face looks funny. If she were anyone else, Gretel would swear she was about to cry.

"Stupid girls." Jill shakes her head. "They should have just waited. That's all they had to do. They would have grown up, and everything would have been all right."

"I'm glad we waited," Gretel says.

They stare at the garage where the two girls died. There's a car parked in it now, and the door is locked, just in case any neighborhood kids get it into their heads to claim a souvenir. But there hasn't been a news story about the incident in days, not even in the town paper, and over at the high school most people have dropped the subject completely. It's only Jill who still comes here, and after tonight, even she won't return. She's glad that the weather is so perfect. The air is mild and wraps around you; it's sweet when you breathe in and when you breathe out.

"Hey," Gretel says. "Look at this." She holds out her arm to show Jill that a firefly has landed on her skin. It blinks a pale yellow light—an SOS. A signal to the soul.

"Should we kill it?" Jill says.

They laugh like crazy at that. Two crazy girls on the sidewalk in the middle of a June night when everyone else in the neighborhood is safe in bed. As they're laughing, the firefly floats away; it rises so high it's impossible to tell where it is among the stars.

"It decided to live," Gretel says.

Some things, after all, are as simple as that.

"Well, good for it." Jill stares up through the trees, even though she knows she'll never see that firefly again. "Good for us," she says.